The Comatose Kids

By Seymour Simckes

SEVEN DAYS OF MOURNING   *(novel & play)*

TEN BEST MARTYRS OF THE YEAR   *(play)*

THE COMATOSE KIDS

SEYMOUR SIMCKES

Illustrated by Mimi Gross Grooms
and A. Joffe

Sections of this novel have appeared in *Fiction*.

This publication is in part made possible with support from the New York State Council on the Arts, and with the cooperation of Teachers and Writers Collaborative and Brooklyn College.

First Edition
Copyright © 1975 by Seymour Simckes
All rights reserved
Typesetting by New Hampshire Composition
    Concord, New Hampshire
Library of Congress Catalog No. 75-10747
ISBN: 0-914590-18-9 (hardcover)
ISBN: 0-914590-19-7 (paperback)

Published by   **FICTION COLLECTIVE**

Distributed by   George Braziller, Inc.
                   One Park Avenue
                   New York, New York 10016

For onion & pecan

We are nihilistic figments, all of us,
suicidal notions forming in God's mind.
___ Franz Kafka

Even the best Doctor lands in Hell.
___ Talmud

Part One

He

had transported them to his own quarters before dawn, pedaled the two of them under a frigid sky, cycling heroically like a pedi-cab boy of Old China, his clients unconscious, semi-blanketed, strapped together face to face inside a wagon attached by rope to his rusted tricycle. To anybody watching, it might have looked as if he were delivering manikins, human antiques. Actually, Doktor Tschisch was kidnapping two patients. One from the City Hospital, the other from the State Asylum.

The boy and girl lay in each other's arms now, in Doktor Tschisch's bed, in the posture the Doktor himself had concocted. Their mouths a mere synapse apart, as though awaiting some crucial message, the girl's hair encasing their two backs in a flow of orange and red, her left arm coddling the boy's head like a discus soon to be thrown as far as Paradise, the sole of his right foot resting upon one of her calves, while her nude slightly-freckled bottom rode his upper right thigh like a saddle, their midriffs joined. Neither of the pair was as yet aware of the other. Hence, for the couple locked in that knot of love it was, apparently, a first encounter.

The Doktor swayed, grimacing with excitement. Scraping his small palms, swallowing bits of food that periodically came up on him. Anxious to inform them of his remarkable guess, of his cure for their unique pathology, Tschisch tickled each of them.

"Sleepyheads! Wake! By corpses I'm not excited. Still tired? In your twenties? Surprise, the main task's done! Gaze at your new Doktor. Imagine how old *he* is! Shocked? I'm *ninety-three*! Up, lovebirds, up!"

Except for a twitch and a snore his patients made no response.

"Okay," burped the Doktor. "So, me first. Then, o, sweethearts, you!" Whereupon Tschisch licked the girl's nearer knee, which jolted away, making room on the bed for the Doktor.

Seated midst his pair, Tschisch squeaked.

"Lovelorns, I am simple! To comprehend me and what I now perform, you need remember almost nothing. Where your eyes? Between two of you I should have *four* pupils! *Inamorati,* I am victim of rare, cruel mumps. Mumps with complications! That's my story! No larger than an obituary! Mumps found me, and left me a child forever. An only one, too! Three elder sisters perished before me. What's me? Simpleton son, surviving greatest European Doktor of his century!''

For a moment Doktor Tschisch sat chewing his cud, catching his breath like a small-toothed hyena, recollecting.

"Sympathy I learned from my Father. He was master at Snap Diagnosis. *Schnell-Diagnose*! Cure he didn't believe in. Well, his school's motto at Vienna was '*Nichts tun*!' The best medicine is no medicine! They divided all gall to two parts. Incurable; self-curable. In either case, Doktor's job was not therapy. Quacks cured, a Doktor *diagnosed*! What concerned my Father was immediately, without consultation, to attach some label on an ailment. Let subsequent autopsy correct him! But no worry, kids. His post-mortems had such style, succulence, proof of each initial snap judgment, throughout Austria-Hungary they were hawked like newspapers! Asia, too—in translation! As he treated strangers, so he treated us. His own children and our Mother, his unfortunate Wife.''

Doktor Tschisch wept, and drank his own tears. Toying with parts of his patients, the boy's nose and the girl's ears, Tschisch sneezed, wheezed, gargled his throat with saliva.

"I couldn't please my Father. He resented my declaming at home Latin as a small boy, though himself all his life had fought for Latin, being himself instructed in Latin and always teaching in that tongue! So when I came down at nine with mumps my Father threw me into bed (not the gentle way I cast you!) and shouted in

Hungarian, 'Mumps is a little disease! Unsophisticated! No aftereffects! Remember? Without *sequelae*! Yet rarities *can* occur! Blocked lungs, deafness, diabetes . . .'

" 'Papa,' I peeped, 'you mean pulmonary infarction, priapism, pancreatitis, meningitis, paralytic poliomyelitis, keratitis, episcleritis, dacryoadenitis, and encephalomyeloradiculoneuritis or Guillian-Barré syndrome?' He yelled back on my face, 'In *your* case I predict sterility! Your tiny testes will swell, then shrivel! You won't beget anything! Just talk!' 'Papa, that's *orchitis*!' 'Exactly,' agreed Father, 'inflammation of your orchid! For that there's no treatment. Only luck!' 'Even if I never leave my bed, Papa?' 'No difference!' 'Papa, won't leeches help?' 'Son, kiss your ball-balls goodbye!' "

Doktor Tschisch fanned himself with both hands. "Well? What would *you* do in my predicament?"

Tschisch's audience answered nothing.

"Me, I waited," continued the Doktor. "While Father made faces at me, I flipped through my favorite magazines and booklets on my sickbed. Kahlbaum on catatonics; Skoda's manual for scoring the music of disease (e.g., drums of pneumonia); Schönlein's innovation, mirrors and lights to investigate eye, throat, esophagus; Wunderlich on renal apoplexy; Kaan (a distant relative) on undersexuality in Latin. Came the critical eighth day, I skimmed Rokitansky's three volumes of anatomy, Virchow's pathology, Müller's magnificent stuff on starfish, sea cucumbers, sharks, the human voice, and genital embryology. Then said my prayers. Would my big mumps now descend to my testicles?

"Alas, they grew," confessed the Doktor. "Almost exploded in my face. With pillows I supported them and beat my head to sleep against my wall. By some miracle, just *one* testicle atrophied to an olive. The other hung normal. Not a potato, but at least an egg! That enraged Father. He cursed me in each language that he knew, in triplets, in sextuplets! 'I'm a Doktor!' he always began mornings, to wake me, prior to heading for his hospital, 'I recognize your case, you're retarded. Look at you! Degenerate, crazy! Admit it. I'll work with you, try my best, against my own medical judgment! Understand? You haven't any coordination. Never dance, don't speak, just cry. Crying you can! That's best! Nobody will guess what you are. That's your only chance. I know what I'm saying, son. I'm a Doktor. Admit it, you're an idiot! Otherwise, today, in your sleep, you'll die!'

"I never admitted it, kids," sighed the Doktor. "Yet I'm still living! Actually, I have my Father to thank for what I am today. He instructed me in compassion."

The Doktor paused to pet the faces of his patients. "All my Father's ways imprinted that lesson. *Compassion.* My Father never spoke to his own patients. Only after they became corpses did he confer with them, address them, soothe, pity. And now, I myself await for you to resurrect so I may confirm my own diagnosis and start therapy. Rise, trust me!"

Before the Doktor had a chance to clean the wax from his ears, the girl bolted from her stupor and began pelting the Doktor in his neck, heart, kidney, and groin. All the while screaming like an ambulance, as though *she* were the one being struck. Upon the Doktor's cries of pain, she stiffened and stared, one hand clasping her lower lip, the other pinching her elbow.

"That's the way," applauded Tschisch, smiling at her. "Protect your beloved. Prove I'm on the right track before I should even turn on my engine! Though I found you in different places, you two aren't strangers, you know one another very well! Somehow you were broken apart, now I brought you together. You're lovers again!"

Doktor Tschisch removed his huge coat and his torn green shirt.

"Let's get to work, kids!"

In

spite of his aches the Doktor took heart. Circling past the sculptured girl, Doktor Tschisch confronted the outstretched boy whose face still was as if tied and bound to death.

"You can't escape me," he grunted. "I'm here to spider-rope your mangled mind. Up roots, acqueducts, gyrations, horns. Across gaps, seamonsters, olives, almonds, pyramids, buttons, saddles, isthmi, bundles, roofs, I won't be satisfied with cramped quarters, I'll jump your cerebral chasms on one leg like a pigeon or a child landing on a sidewalk game, a rock in his hand!"

Kissing the silent boy, the Doktor checked for any small progress. None so far.

"No matter how complex you are," resumed the Doktor, "it's no tragedy. Complexity is love. Love's a circuitous cat, sets its eyes away from you but fixes you with its ears. There she is! Back again! Your beloved. Reborn. I'm just here to tell you it's time to cry over spilled milk. We all feel what's in our hands only after its weight is gone. Now you can appreciate her! Yesterday, your love knew not your whereabouts and you knew not hers. Today, I've joined you together like a dream to its owner, like air to lungs, and shall now become the board you two may see-saw upon for the rest of your lives, for I am the fulcrum, I am your point of leverage permitting both your freedoms and your eternal attachment!"

At that point the boy in bed farted. Likewise the standing girl. Afterward the Doktor himself.

"That reminds me," coughed Doktor Tschisch, removing his cordoroy pants. "Last night I had a dream. I was back in Vienna, Head of Psychiatric Ward of *Allgemeines Krankenhaus,* curing my patients left and right, not merely observing them like other neurological monkeys, yet two patients wouldn't respond and I condemned them in my heart, committing both to hopelessness and death, wouldn't touch them lest I myself sink from control and out of the game like a hit billiard ball, and all Vienna was spinning from laughter, mocking the amateur Doktor who couldn't baffle two Comatose Kids. My psychology was too simple. I collapsed all theory and practice to two principles. The trouble was, I wasn't certain which had knocked them down, *repetition* or *contradiction*! Until a stranger visited my Ward, claiming he wished to hear how each of my patients lost his mind so he might pick the manner suitable for himself.

" 'Stable types like me have that privilege!' he spouted. 'Yes, Doktor? I don't *come* sick like a nuisance. I *leave* sick, *stay* sick, like those Kids of yours, eh? Where are they? How did *they* come so numb? From watching your magic? Is your knowledge that narcotic? Are they here for political reasons? You investigated? What are their names? Know *anything* about them? Quit joking! This your method, smoking cigars while two saints coagulate? I'll write you up in a newspaper! Have you ousted! You're more dangerous to your patients than an open window!' And he farted in my face, something that isn't done in Vienna, in professional circles, even today.

"Suddenly, lovesicks, I was inspired. Galloping to my two dishrags, I yodeled: 'Hey! Your mutual madness means love!' Suddenly, like magic, my two unconscious kids jumped like clothes in wind, both yapping at once from a vortex of realization!"

Wheeling like a beast, Tschisch dragged the stiff girl into bed where, once more, he weaved together the two bodies of his patients. The girl, come viciously alive, attempted to extricate herself by spitting on the Doktor and the boy, but Tschisch forced a union.

"Tying me to a corpse?" screamed the girl. "That your idea of medicine?"

"He's just waiting for you to confess affection," said

Tschisch. Taking a small pencil from behind his ear, the Doktor planted it in the boy's left hand. Immediately the boy began scribbling on the girl's back.

Though it tickled her the girl gasped. "Is he some unemployed circus freak? Untie me!"

"Not yet," said the Doktor. "Isn't he the same boy?"

"What boy?" moaned the girl slipping over the bed's edge toward the floor, her green eyes lapsed into emptiness.

"The one you adored!"

"I never adored anyone."

"Is that so?" said the Doktor. "Why you hugging him?"

"What are you talking about?" insisted the girl. "I'm hugging nothing."

"What about me?" asked Tschisch. "Can you see me at least?"

"Nobody."

"Look again!"

Winking, Doktor Tschisch shoved his eyeball against hers.

"When a man's face is along a woman's," explained the Doktor, "their eyes jump out of line. The eyes of Modigliani's women are not on the same level because he's caught them at a time of intimacy. So, girl. Is this the eye you remember? Am *I* your boy?"

She slapped his face with her forehead.

"Hoo-hoo," he whistled. "Thanks for the hint. I won't wedge again between you and your beloved here!"

At that, as the girl still struggled to free herself, the boy's eyes opened.

"Wait, wait," said the Doktor. "Here he comes!"

As though not talking but scraping a carrot, as though he were a pencil on a page, the boy emerged from his coma voicing, "Seagulls maggots."

Doktor Tschisch clapped his hands. The girl smothered her ears, droning her own ditty. "My Lover plays organ. My Lover, flute. I'm just backward, I play lute!"

"What a couple," commented Tschisch, waving kisses at them both. "My job's almost over!"

"Sky sick with worms," sputtered the boy.

"My birthdays tumble," countered the girl, "jumble, toss. I say nothing, never cross. What's all the ruckus, why the song? We've been forgotten, done no wrong!"

"Ah," nodded the Doktor. "More you love, crazier you are! My cat takes my seat the second I'm gone. That's how fast insanity replaces love!"

All of a sudden a gray bulging cat, hoisting himself via a dead vine, entered the broken window, made a piercing quack like an overexcited duck, then chattered as if it had sighted birds in a tree, not humans on a bed.

"Pay no attention to him," advised the Doktor. "He's my child. But a nonentity! What can we expect from animals? A horse spends half his brain on his nose. Not man or woman. You have other purposes. You are in each other's pockets, in each other's dreams. When I first saw you, though, you were wrecks! With blue faces, cold feet, even arcs of senility round your irises. Believe me, the two of you looked like congenital idiots!"

"Shut up!" said the girl in a crouch. "I have no qualms pulling your pants down in the street. I'll hold your looloo like a leash!"

In his enjoyment Doktor Tschisch spun the girl around to face the bedridden boy. The moment her knee grazed the boy's waist, both patients scampered from each other like infant mice. Buried under his sheet, the boy snored. Stuck to a wall, the girl hissed. The cat, as though rebuking the Doktor for taking on such ungrateful patients, vomited at Tschisch's feet.

"Hey," complained the Doktor. "All of you! Stop posing like lunatics! Hysteria's good only once in a while!"

Tschisch dug his thumb into the boy's backside, his pinky into the girl's stomach, his shoe into the cat's mouth.

"Actually," continued the Doktor, "I once recited a five hour lecture on this, inside an asylum for hysterical kids at Prague, as a patient there. I mean, all of us are placed in the same uneasy spot, watching our caretakers transform in voice, face, character, from anger. That frightens a child, teaches him a lesson. Not just that he must imitate his unloved as well as loved parent. More. When pushed to choose, he selects the extreme. Because fake has proved more powerful. Yes, everybody's tempted to live on a swing, now friend now foe, from argument to reconciliation. Enough snippets! You're cockeyed from passion. I took you here not for the purpose of keeping you separate. Hurry, kids. Make love!"

Doktor Tschisch had lost his patients to sleep. Uninsulted, he crawled quickly into bed with the boy, playing a second snail concealed for some shared reason.

Why shouldn't Tschisch rest too? Hadn't he earned it? Hadn't he uncorked each patient in an amazing jiffy, punctured the girl's long-standing stupor, roused the boy from his coma until he actually spoke language? The instant the Doktor slumbered, his mind was at peace.

Not so the sleeping minds of his patients.

The boy imagined he had been removed from his grave, as though somebody dear to him requested to see his face again before worms got there. Nothing else was clear. He couldn't understand what had caused his ability to speak, or his inability. He was at a loss to recall himself. He only hoped he was caught in one of his own stories.

The girl realized one thing. Horrified after her rape by that creature, she determined to seek her suicide at the appropriate moment.

In any case, while the small room slept its mixture of ease and nightmare, the horizon outdoors mechanically cut another sun and the cold new day rose like a patient uninformed of his cancer.

Under

Tschisch's influence the frozen girl had another nightmare. But this time, after she somehow killed herself, she lay high on a table set for autopsy, only one hour beyond the date of her expiration. With her Coroner in his button-free overcoat snoozing alongside her like an extra passenger.

In other words, she saw that her degradation did not end with her death. In spite of her suicide she was still treated as a fake, and would be carted from asylum to asylum. Unless her Coroner chose to revive her. For what purpose? To kill her his own way! Slice her awkwardly into small bits for sale as toothpicks.

Suddenly she felt the Coroner's body move. She heard him drop like a monkey from his bar and grope for his instruments. Then, not locating them, he hastened back to her as if deciding that she didn't deserve anything better than bare hands. In her desperation the girl was unable to watch anymore. But the moment the Coroner touched her, she peeped, "I'm Chinese, from Hangchow!" as though such a disclosure, at the last minute, might protect her somehow.

The Coroner answered, "I know that. I tell from the way you use your hands! Where you should point with a pinky, you employ your thumb. Only a native says *fly-fly egg* when he means *bomb*! Hey, was the smell of Hangchow same as Shanghai? All cabbage and shit?"

"I like you," the girl heard herself say, in her nakedness. "You're the only one who believes I'm Chinese."

For some reason, that angered the Coroner. Disregarding her affectionate overture, he hauled her to the floor. There, caught against the red linoleum, the girl watched him damage her. While he inserted his fingers into her, breaking her everywhere like Samson at the pillars, she regretted having confessed her Oriental origins.

Years ago, when she first admitted she was a Chinese girl, her Doctor laughed in her face, pointing at her flamingo hair as if that meant she was a liar, that her woe was just hysteria and hullabaloo. At that time she insisted she had been manhandled in China, raped, tricked, trafficked. But, patting her freckled cheeks, he praised her imagination.

Her own Mother once slapped her face on the street, for supposedly lying in public about bleeding to death.

That whack, on the day of her initial menstruation, made it impossible for her to trust anybody but herself.

But, after all, that woman wasn't her actual Mother. Just a parent by adoption. From the start, then, the girl was trapped, she could never run away because Chinese custom prevented her from using her foster name outside the household. The truth was, the girl was but an investment for old age when her so-called Mother, a ballroom dancer, couldn't perform for strangers anymore. So, really, she had no name. Yet, without one, she knew herself well enough. She carried her own luggage, didn't need any Prince Charmings around. Her asylum days were over. She required no proof of her recovery in order to kill herself. She could have been anything, even an ancient Hittite, except a girl shipped from China to a Hell where she had to take orders from everyone but herself. Suicide was her sole rescue.

Now, however, that her Coroner had dismembered her completely, she pitied herself.

"Are you going to bury me like this?" she asked. "Can't you put me together first?"

"What?" coughed the Coroner. "I've eaten your tongue and kidneys already. It's too late!"

The girl wept and bargained, as if for the final time in her life, "If you help me, I'll scrub your floors with my face!"

By the end of her nightmare, the girl saw that she would never be herself again. Her Doctors would now spread their false dope on her, claim she sucked all comers, men or women, like mango pits. So, as her mind whirled doomward, her flesh stiffened like frozen soup.

The boy, too, was at a loss how to reconstruct himself. With Doktor Tschisch breathing down one of his ears, he struggled to imagine what was wrong with his mind. But the trouble was, his brain felt like something borrowed. In a few seconds he would have to return it to some other person. To a brain so badgered, a string of lamplights appeared like a bridge spanning water. After intense self-scrutiny, all the boy could come up with was that he wasn't the only individual in danger. His Father too had death in his blood. Even though three Doctors diagnosed just a cough. The boy, *now*, knew better. Some Angel of Death, disguised as a Greek thug, was around. If the boy didn't outwit that bum in time, he'd be cheated of his Father. To save a life he'd have to maneuver through Death's fingers like a seagull. His Father must not get out of bed! Once he stood up, his heart would snap like costume jewelry. The boy fought to awaken, but lethargy sat on his eyes and erased his mind.

Meanwhile Doktor Tschisch, stuck in bed, was actually on his way to the Garden of Eden, his reward for having created, not just saved, two loves. According to Tschisch's intricate dream of glory, the entire community of Angels was applauding the Doktor. Not to mention God Himself.

Yes, Doktor Tschisch had no problems now. He had absconded with the right specimens from America's junk yard. Celery so limp, sooner discarded the better. Who could complain? He was safe as long as he kept the boy and girl from reaching any answer about themselves other than the one Tschisch had prepared. That meant cracking *all* mirrors of memory.

Naturally the Doktor saw no need to justify himself before any world of law or medicine. He had his sister's image as his amends. Good for her was good for him. All through life he maintained communication with that dead girl. Now was no exception. Now was the game's last move, the sequence that won. Tschisch's childhood lasted long enough.

He hadn't instigated his experiment on the spur of this moment. He was aware he was initiating a *folie à trois.* No snap judgment here. He realized he was forcing others to share his craziness. Putting the girl and boy together was, for Tschisch, not a gamble. His entire existence pointed toward this instant when the two kids would swim in his words and clinch like rejoined nerves.

Provided, of course, Doktor Tschisch worked quickly. Because he himself was dying. As soon as the sun sank three times the Doktor would fall into death's ultimate arms. Before then, Tschisch wanted those kids cooing over each other like plump pigeons. By the time they'd discover his trick the Doktor would be gone. Back, at last, to his sister of Paradise.

Therefore, Doktor Tschisch and his sleep-prone patients had something in common. Although each nurtured a different dream now, all three imagined themselves expired.

"Good

afternoon," clarified Doktor Tschisch sprawled under the window, kneeling comfortably with his head sideways on the sill, a camel at his inscrutable ease, glorified by the noonday sun. "Your luck! Today you learn your lives. *All facts!*"

The Doktor's patients sat squarely before him like students.

Except that the girl, more interested in her own mouth than Tschisch's lecture, was biting her lips inside and out until they bled, as if that could make the Doktor stop talking.

As for the boy, he was unable to locate the Doktor altogether. However painstakingly he rotated his vision, the pieces remained miles apart. Something, probably the Doktor's coat, lumpy and blue, with large safety pins for buttons, curled from the floor like a sick flower. Whereas down from the ceiling hung two spindly items gray as twilight which the boy identified not as lightbulbs but the Doktor's eyes. Meanwhile, the entire room throbbed as if injured. Under such conditions, the boy was almost certain that the Doktor was the shadow of his own chair.

"Together now," encouraged Tschisch. "Let's figure your both biographies out."

"*Monsieur*," waved the girl, her face monstrous. "Why are we in your ham hands alone? I had others to tease me, ask me for a dance, force me chew chemicals! Where's my whole world? How come just you are in charge of us? *Your cock's showing*!"

Checking his fly with one finger the Doktor agreed.

"Yes, otherwise things can slip from our hands completely."

"Cover up!" ordered the girl like royalty. "I can still see your little bundle."

"Kids," hiccupped Tschisch. "Go backward now. You must rehearse what you know. Deepen. Parenthesize your situation. Smell each fragrance!"

"What's wrong, bald-ears?" she needled. "You lost?"

"No means," Tschisch snorted. "We're safe like pedestrians in Budapest of 1890. I hitched streetcars then so padded back and front, no complaint existed of anybody crushed under wheel. Whereas America's record was scandal. Begin! Don't you want your life's stories back?"

"What?" asked the boy talking to his feet.

"Say nothing," advised the girl. "Unless he tortures you!"

"That's it," blurted Tschisch. "Aid one another, starting from scratch. Weren't you two half-orphans the day you were born? But who of you had the Father fixation? Who the Mother's? By now I myself am confused. You come from same puzzle. Fit like enzymes! Answer me. Who is which?"

Not his patients, but Tschisch himself half an hour later, snapped the dry silence by slamming his sneakers flat.

"Boy," he howled. "You image your Father perfectly! Remember him? Thin, elegant, but bankrupt? Poet of Argentina whose work showed up only on Yiddish newspapers? That poisoned your Mother. Right after your birth, once she caught your boy face, she knew you'd copy your Father. Another marvelous mannered fiasco! So in her hospital bed, she died. That's the trouble, boy. You were vulnerable like an opened apple from the start. All you had for a God was an unlucky Father. He was your whole life. You grew to care for him like your own infant. But despite your crazy devotion, his dream for recognition broke up. He walked everywhere crying. All the way to Brazil. Then Honduras, Mexico, America. With you hankering to think, sing, write like him. Wanting to wear his striped suit. That was your ambition. But behind your back, suddenly he too was dead. Under his bedcovers. You were stymied, absolutely locked out. A mourner with enough money on you to last a month. At eighteen, what could you do? Naturally you fell in love. Thank God. To a girl with imagination. Her!"

"Where did you get all this crap?" complained the girl.

"Remember now what snatched your heart from you?" asked the Doktor. "Her orange hair? Her story of escape from her Mongolian orphanage? No worry. Whatever the foundation was for your love, it was not despair simply. To the contrary. The basis was uncanny, your mutual ability to interpret one another. You saw she was a woman too soon. In order to survive she chose herself already at age three! Alas, because of her harsh Mother she decided on secrecy. Keeping her doors closed always, keeping all waiting for her. But she never came. Except for you. Since you knew what it felt to be her. To others she was insane. And madness makes enemies quicker than bees make honey. But you caught her timing. Others thought her a piece of wood for she was so slow, particularly her Mother. That lady was too busy for her. She couldn't wait around for her to speak, think, eat. Poor girl, everything was taken away from her before she had a chance, as if nothing in the world would interest her whereas, in truth, she was a child so dumbfounded by all she saw and couldn't touch that, hours, she could stare at the shadow of an insect. Or at just the wind, how it dried her tears, tossed her hair, opened her clothes. Her excitement was ignored. As far as Mother was concerned the girl could not respond. Hence in dark concealed closets the girl would whirl and howl, slap her own face and collapse backward like a

war casualty. No wonder Mother smuggled her onto a
ship with instructions to transfer her from immigration
to immigration, under care of a few sailors until they
tired of her. By the time she met you, boy, her life was
so bleak that, to give it any meaning, she'd make a
battle-cry over a straw. She was a mourner at her own
funeral. It's a good thing you made love the moment your
paths crossed. How you came apart, that's another story.
Anyway, for our purpose today it's enough. Congratulations! I'm your missing Papa and Mama. Okay? Kiss
again!"

"You ramble like a child," spat the girl as the boy's
bewildered head slumped between his knees.

"That's me," acknowledged Tschisch. "From foot to
face!" lifting his toes to the girl's eyes as though to
perform some card trick. "Scratch. Watch them fan
open and curl back. Babinski invented the test, my
Father's neurological rival. Scratch my toes and see I
have reflexes of a child. Either that or brain damage!"

"If this is some nursery I'm leaving!" said the girl.
"Are you in your second childhood or third?"

"Okay," submitted the Doktor blowing his nose out
the window. "Me again for the last time. Afterward,
kids, the bed is yours!"

"Why

was I always taken for a child? Mumps is not the whole answer. Already before mumps I was multiple child. I had to replace all my missing sisters. Poor victims. Their only mistake, a smidgen. A chromosomal technicality!

"Kids, my first sister was *amauritic.* After the Greek word for darkness. She came here a born idiot. With reddish dots in her blue eyes to signal that her death was on the way. My second was a so-called *cri-du-chat* case. She mewed like a cat as an infant. She was buried after her first birthday.

"Do not forget. This was the days when asylums everywhere, from England to Russia, claimed that all Jews were predisposed to not only idiocy but leprosy, abnormally sized heads and tongues, prognathous jaws, harelip, cleft palate, goitre, deaf mutism, epilepsy, even *icthyosis*!

28

"So, kids, after each grotesque arrival and departure of my sisters, my Father's popularity diminished. He was forced to move from Vienna to Budapest, to Venice, to Prague, to Trieste.

"My last sister, though, was no freak. She was unbreakable, wild, gorgeous. But with one Achilles heel. Her rule was she must never be examined. She thought of a Doktor as somebody who finds you out and condemns you, handing you over to authorities for extermination. But in 1871 she was caught, my darling sister. In Berlin. Remember that one year war, Prussia against France? France had a beating. Even a French museum was shelled! So, to compensate, she called Prussia Mongolian!

"At once my Father's other rival, Doktor Virchow, instigated a national census. To prove Prussia was Teutonic, millions of school kids were clinically examined. Many scared from their wits. Alas my dark sister dyed her eyes and her hair with blueberry jam. But in Virchow's presence she collapsed and was expelled outright as a fake.

"Afterward, from age nine onward her body hardly developed. Her appetite altogether vanished. Throughout her teens I fed her like an animal. I adored her. Watched her like the hawk. Once, when she was eighteen, she came to me all naked and asked, 'Can you see anything?' Kids, what was there to see? She had become what was termed in the literature of that day a Chloritic Maiden. Yet Virchow never cited her case in his classic 'Aortic Hypoplasia with Contracted Heart in Chloritic Maidens.'

"To her end my sweetheart never menstruated, as though she had no desire to be awakened unto female life. She wasted. Barely slept. Sang nights at the top of her consumptive lungs. Vomited, refusing any cure, her nails so brittled they snapped in wind, her skin flaky, indifferent to her own pains. A frenzied companion for prostitutes and punks, she gnawed peach pits though her teeth dropped out in the process. Father announced, '*Anorexia nervosa, hysterica apepsia, cachexia.* Fatal!' And abandoned his university post. Amid an endless weeping fit following her funeral, I developed mumps!"

Frantically, with her hands and feet, the girl applauded.

"Thanks," said Tschisch and sucked the tears from his fingers. "That, lovers, has been my life. A perpetual motion machine made up of childhoods. Ever hear of Vigotsky, or Piaget? Those big-shot Professors construed me ten when I was already twenty! Both interviewed me, copied out my every word, baby talk included. By Doktor Freud's door years later, I posed as a juvenile obsessed with psychoanalytic theory, quoting it non-stop like Scriptures. After a couple months Freud thought he cured me. My reward? Carrying important personal correspondence for his inner circles. Rank to Jung, Jung to Adler, Adler to Tausk, Tausk to Freud! Forever on my bike. Special delivery! A thirty-year-old behaving as a two-year-old. At forty-five, in a Viennese public garden, I participated like other children in Moreno's psychodrama for kiddies, messing up the show with Latin monologues. Believe me. No clinic of Europe had ever imagined such a case before my time. A child within a child within a child! Always going backwards!

"But my height of childhood came inside Poland when I was assigned, a man of sixty, to a children's section of my concentration camp. In those days I wore a bedspread for my outfit. It was no joke though. They worked me like a kettle. At war's end I recruited up and down for volunteers to testify at trials. My entire camp laughed at its talking bedspread, its baby. 'Shit! *Shmonses*! Idiot! It's all over. What does it matter now?' De Gaulle visited us. Picked me out, declared me youngest survivor of any furnace of Europe. Ordered my name rostered so his Government adopt and educate me for nothing. Instead I came to America with an empty satchel and a final dream.

"Customs, of course, investigated me, the tiny orphan traveller. Suspecting a false bottom somewhere on me. While I sat sobbing for some rich American Uncle who might stuff my life with gold! But the two of you are my single riches. From my guile of Rumania to my American sneakers my entire life has prepared our meeting. Now my sacred sister rivets me to you. No longer must I choke for her like an alley cat. Instead I can behold her again in my arms. You are testimony of her power. She is your momentum. Let love now be your simple goal, human flesh your food and only truth. Confess your passion of as old. Through you I achieve completion. *Enfin*, adult!"

"Stick his lungs with a fork," commented the girl. "It's too dangerous to wait for his suicide!"

In a voice of some distant bird the boy recited from his chair, "Is semen of mine on your bum? Let me wipe it off."

Staring at his toes, biding his time like a professional, Doktor Tschisch simply noised his favorite Slavic filler, "*Mnye, mnye, mnye.*"

"Cracked pot," interrupted the girl. "Scram, we can guard ourselves!"

"Very encouraging," hummed Tschisch. "Your other Doktors would startle to hear my accomplishment. *We* she says! Already you are inseparable!"

She corrected him. "*We* means *me*! Anyone with education knows that. Think you can take us for some ride? Where are we anyway? This place a cemetery?"

"*We* means lovers strayed from each other. You and you. Caught by an oscillation of misunderstanding. Your unconscious faces taught me that. Am I tricking you? Am I some wangler? Monster? Crook? Rotten, careless to witness love at any cost for I had none in my life? Here is proof that I did not invent your relationship!"

Doktor Tschisch drew a long strand of red hair from the boy's pajama sleeve which matched exactly, in color and length, the girl's hair.

"Like insects in a bush," declared the Doktor. "Tangled in a man's flesh, love's evidence is everywhere!"

As though wounded the girl howled. Then stiffened like a trained mimist suspended nowhere.

The boy spun the strand around his thumb repeating, "Control yourself." And sunk to sleep.

Sensing the dangers ahead of him Doktor Tschisch crawled under the bed and made new plans.

Before

entirely dying, the half-sunk sun broke the girl's stupor open. Caught inside those ambiguous flames, she panicked. Her physician was absent. All she saw was that slim boy slouched in a lopsided wicker chair, scratching a tiny pencil across his pajamas, fiercely absorbed, at work despite his mishap. The empty bed hung now at a weird angle, as though some sleeper there intended to slide into the sea a corpse. Hence, she heaved with menstrual pain and criss-crossed amok from wall to wall. Flying a jeopardized kite, it would seem. Or enacting the plight of a trapped sparrow who couldn't find her exit to the sky.

The boy continued to scribble over his pajamas. His way of arguing against Tschisch. By sticking close to his own stories he might avoid becoming someone he never was. Now, crumpled up as though his goal were to mend his clothes, the boy calculated his figments. Sorted his events while his mind yet worked. Perhaps he was the one who, afraid of another disappointment, had walked out of his hospital before the fourth or fifth operation was ready for his blind eyes?

"I'm up," celebrated Tschisch, his head emerging beneath the slanted bed like something that had no need of sleep.

"It see-saws now! My medical texts at the middle solve anything. Now you may exchange love past for love present. The sun isn't still down. Play. I won't watch. To bed!"

His two patients stared at each other from a distance.

The Doktor whispered to the alarmed girl, "Isolde, you can worship your passion now. Tristram has arrived safely!"

She mumbled, "My name ain't Isolde."

The Doktor beckoned the baffled boy. "Samson! Guess who is upon you? Red and freckled as ever! See Delilah?"

The boy wanted very much to see something clearly. But couldn't. His lids collapsed. The world's pigments around him made too much noise.

Tschisch kneaded back the boy's vision. "For once," gargled the Doktor. "Recall what she is?"

Through Tschisch's tutelage the impaired boy noted a huge tree with palm-like leaves engulfing half the room. Hordes of giant flies, or bees. And that wild girl moping at a cracked window, staring out or in at him.

"Any idea now?" asked the Doktor.

"She dances," the boy said.

The Doktor burped, "With her bad posture?"

"Her wrists float," the boy insisted, demonstrating.

Before Tschisch had a chance to question her, the girl stretched and spun, snaked, leaped, bobbed, her eyes enlarged and flashing like a berserk octopus.

"Talented kids!" said Tschisch. "*He* writes, *she* dances. *Me*? My Father could be Aristotle but I'd end up town Coroner! You two can afford perfection. Kiss tongues!"

"Castrate your cat," the girl said.

"You remind me of my sister," admitted Tschisch. "Could kiss you myself."

"Who's stopping you?" she asked and exposed her long bum.

Tschisch hardly bent as he smacked lips and teeth against her orange flesh. "Ooooo," he chanted. "Without compare. Boy, try it yourself. That you can't forget!"

The boy faltered, "I'm not certain where I am."

"With her. You are her beloved."

"My bracelet," the girl corrected. "Can't look at him. He makes my eyes boil."

Tschisch murmured, "Passion, such passion."

Fanning herself by shaking her head the girl whined, "Scum! Who needs you? I can maim your neck off. Chop you as you sleep. Don't you know my name? Can't you read?"

"I don't follow charts," said Tschisch. "They blind

me to other chances. Who cares for names? Hear me call any of my sweet sisters by name?"

"Where is she?" the boy asked, confused, his ears half blocked. "Is that your sister?"

"Expect me to kiss a freak like him!" she said. "If he's not dumb he's deaf or blind."

"And what are you, girlie?" asked Tschisch. "Remember your last ward? Would some college boy adopt or marry a ghost like you? Thank me you weren't raped down a staircase or kidnapped by tragic pranksters! Ask what your Doktors all thought of you."

The girl sprang, strangely comforted by the Doktor's conversation. "You read my chart?"

"Kidnapped? Are we kidnapped?" the boy requested quietly.

"Here's a paper bag," said Tschisch, removing it from his back pocket like a handkerchief. "This'll clear your heads, give you energy for kissing. Breathe right into it. Then inhale your own air. Afterward we can make a short walk outside to the corner. In the dark."

Tschisch's patients, for the first time, gazed at one another close up, either seeking some cock-eyed clue of recognition or exchanging some signal of escape.

The Doktor sighed. "It's seeping in, how much I care for you. Here, you must have lungs like a hippo, boy, and suck like a whore. Create a vacuum. Your love watches you now as if you were a building on fire."

The slow boy reached for the bag, crushed the top in his fist, brought the paper mouthpiece to his lips and blew like a suicidal musician. His face squashed as though he had just come from the womb. In fact, he might have passed Tschisch's neurological test if the girl hadn't caught the bloated bag between her palms in one explosive slap.

"I was expecting that," the Doktor said and presented the boy with another bag from his pocket.

The capricious girl usurped it at once and stuck it high on her ear, exhaling grotesquely and winking at Tschisch through a loop in her curtain of hair.

Tschisch re-aligned their faces, pressing the boy's brow against the girl's. "Hoot when you see just one eye."

Immediately the boy whispered, "I do."

"What?" said the girl.

"It's like an island without water," the boy said, delighted by his returned vision. "Like a small lake with one huge fish inside. Can you see mine?"

"Always," she said.

"So why aren't you married?" asked Tschisch.

"Because we just met," she said.

"Faker," the Doktor said.

As if handed an order, the boy shuffled to his bed, carefully separated a pillow from its case, inserted his feet into the sack as though that were his trousers, and fainted face down.

Now the girl hooted. "That's how you woo? Here's the better way," sailing up and landing down on her partner's rump, flogging him with her fists.

"Making love already?" peeped the Doktor. "I'll hide hind my tree. And soy beans have!"

Stung

to her bone, insulted, frantic, gyrating like a hornet she attacked the Doktor.

He ran across and along the room.

As she chased him, Tschisch's seemingly pregnant cat loomed over the sink basin, yelping like a creature with a wrung neck, then slumped against the faucet as if poisoned by the mere sight of the Doktor's patients.

Tschisch continued his dodge. "Explore him yourself. His prior love won't be such mystery if you touch around with no shame!" Circling back. "Help him, you're a Doktor now, allow yourself anything. Can I push his legs apart for you? Just a beginning. What you want!" Turning on her, catching her in his arms, both of them spilling like clowns.

"One kiss there," predicted Tschisch. "He'll stand up another man."

Out of breath but hugging her Doktor she said, "You do it yourself."

"But I'm not his girl."

She tossed, "Start. I'm next. I promise!"

Tschisch, making no fuss, nibbled at the boy's exposed penis as though it were a desert flower.

Her eyes by the act, the girl commented, "Stinks like rotten mushroom."

Tschisch said, "I watched sex of all kinds. Paraplegic even. Your turn, lady!"

The girl swirled off.

"Never! That thing's blotched! I have my own grocery!"

"Come. Be gentle. Wheedle, nuzzle, lick."

"Is that what yours is like? Stained, marked all over?"

The Doktor squeaked.

"I'm victim from mumps. Remember? His has nothing to do with mine. He's normal. Hurry."

"Not me!"

"You just made me a promise. Keep it. Like my sister!"

The girl whimpered.

"You took a nut's word? Go live among liars!"

"Emergency!" Tschisch warned.

"I'm sick too."

"Look at him," said Tschisch. "Look at yourself."

She lowered her face to the boy's bare sex, halted, then sputtered, "It's not fair. He doesn't know what we're doing to him."

"Sighting your orange hair across his testicles won't anger him. Anyway—everything you say, he hears!"

"You're sicker than both of us!"

Tschisch smacked her face. She slapped his.

"See?" said the Doktor. "We need a referee. Wake him up."

However, the boy woke on his own. Sighing, "I knew a girl who couldn't control her kite."

"What color was the kite?" the Doktor asked, not anxious for the boy's amnesia to wear off.

The boy was stuck.

Excited, the girl pointed one leg up and rooted her other limbs to the floor as if at a crucial moment of hopscotch. "Can I tell him his *real* story now?"

"Of course," said Tschisch, as though the news were good and she his colleague.

"His back ached so much, he never sat in a chair."

A man of opportunity, Tschisch knuckled the boy's upper and lower back.

The girl honked. Cartwheeling.

"Face it, kid. You weren't normal. Know how you sat? Head first!"

The boy glared.

Tschisch played mum.

"You were a worse freak walking. If any sun came out, you crumpled. Grabbed your face in queer ways—as your shield from life. Always palming your teeth or ears. With half a hand in your mouth. Otherwise, you'd yell your head off."

"False," the boy gasped.

Tschisch kept possum.

"As for talking, impossible," she summed up. "You gestured instead. Except in your sleep. No wonder your Father died, kid. On account of you! You run-down jerk! I'd kick you off any assembly line fast. Quit hanging on!"

The boy made, finally, his own speech, hardly able to breathe, his lips almost glued. "In control I rejoice. In its loss, she!"

"He's on his kite again," the girl explained. "His Pa's in Paris. His Ma in Rome. But he's nowhere. Not even home!"

"I always kept touch with my dancer," spoke the boy, his fingers softly cupping his lips. "Yanking my string. I push art from life. My work grotesque. Me not."

"In life we all gamble till we lose," she contradicted. "Turn, freak. Don't look what I'm going to do to you."

As if encircled by Nazis the skinny boy howled.

She poked his shin with her foot.

The Doktor proclaimed, "It's darkness enough. Come, your first kiss can wait. I'll open the door."

Part Two

Outdoors

Tschisch's patients felt like escaped zoo animals unable to separate any more their freedom from their captivity. Like pots boiling without water. Confused, breathless, exhausted, without kilter, their last speck of soul snapping, having no target to shoot at except themselves. The boy in his white multi-penciled hospital uniform and the girl in her flowing misshaped asylum gown, both ogled the common darkness as if they had never before seen such a thing. Meanwhile, a patient on each arm, Doktor Tschisch, surmounting all their worries, their pains, their panic, swayed softly in the safe middle, spanning a sea of crags and monsters.

The three of them looped together. Smothered in one green quilt blanket like participants at some ceremony of somnabulism. Their procession was measured in

inches, each step an eternity—so as not to tilt their
shaky consciousness. They were like slow-moving cats
about to have sex. When saliva and horrendous gurgles
ooze from their mouths, they rub foreheads, scrutinizing one another's features, and give the impression that
if humans studied each other that long for any reason
they'd go blind.

Actually, half a block behind, trailing despite his own
serious nausea, Tschisch's sick ocelot cat stuck to his job
as witness, down curbs, through shrubbery, under
parked vehicles, his tarnished eyes for lanterns leading
him infallibly on, his purpose not yet knocked out of
him though the night's sky lost its moon and all its stars.

The boy was desperate. In his petrified imagination
he considered himself caught on the street again in the
hands of a Greek schemer, God's courier of Death,
someone to buttonhole him at the crucial moment and
keep him away from his dying Father, put him out of
action, discredit him as an absent-minded Messiah.
Having scanned most of his stories, about outcasts,
dwarfs, castrated troublemakers, lunatic asylums that
also functioned as hotels, landlords evicting tenants
from doghouses and sewers, the boy was certain that
what fit himself factually was his trio tale of a Father,
his Son, and the Devil come between.

At this moment he heard the Greek's voice luring
him. "Can you help me out, kid? I'm stuck for dough."

Wading in dark water up to his throat the boy
propelled himself with terror. "Somebody came up lame

on me, kid. Know what I mean? He didn't pay the whole amount for an abortion. I could get it back. But don't like to put the finger on anybody, unless it requires it! I just look to approach, palm what I can, bet on anything. As for broads, can't pump anymore. No wind, kid. Have to suck 'n chew! Know the worst I had? Alcoholic! Slipped her a saw buck to drink by herself. Waited by my television in my hotel room. She showers drunk. Then, in her leopard panties, nails my neck, stares into my head and says, 'Shut up!' What was she up to? Where's my alibi, kid, if she jumps my window? Destroyed!

"Finally, my opinion she wants. Some creep actually asked her for keeps! Should she take him? 'That's your jurisdiction!' I answer, and scram in my blue pajamas. I don't need tantrums. If I lug a woman home Mum asks, 'Who she?' Mum likes to bathe me herself and scrub my hair. She hates my fag masseur, on account I'm free with tips, favors, contacts, angles, one-shot deals, hoaxes. Hey, wanna witness for each other? Cry *Ouch*! at fake accidents for back pains? Scalp on sport stubs? My softest take was some old fart. Buddy, smack in public, with two cops around, this nut hands out free cash. I request two grand for my hospitalized son. But already the dope's broke. Next morn I'm first at his bank. He offers me a single grand. I put a lousy face on. To show I could really use the other half. That upsets the bum. Backtrack, right? Week later, the guy is cleaned out. No car fare. I say in my baritone voice, 'Here's fifty bucks!' Then knock his balls and temple.

Croak him for good. Hey, kid. Could you make it up to me. The fifty? How about it? Stake me for hospitality sake?"

"Just to that small corner and back," the Doktor explained. "Unless you wish to stay here for your wedding. Canopy we have. Yes, boy? Could you take her tonight without any headache? As former and future bride?"

"I don't know her," the boy stumbled his quarter step, looking for the missing Greek.

"What about you?" Tschisch asked, shimmying the girl's wrist. "Can you re-accept him with no convulsion or doubt? Your old new groom?"

"If you make him hang out any longer he's through."

"Worried you'll be a young widow, lady?"

At that the boy dug up a pencil from his pajama pocket and scrawled something vertically down his sleeve.

"Turtle," warned the girl, her neck hooked over the boy's busy pencil. "If you crap again on me, I'll slam your eyeballs flat! Stop writing!"

Concentrating on what he *almost* recalled about himself, the boy mumbled, "You shut up, please. To you I'm a blank."

The girl cockadoodled, galloping her scales from alto to soprano. "How can I forget your mind? It was a net that never let my fish of passion set one egg inside! You nit-picker!"

"Shell yourself," the boy answered, not knowing what he meant.

The Doktor examined the boy's pajama scroll by the yellow streetlight. "What language is this? Not Spanish? What are you up to?"

"He's hopeless. Open his head. Look inside. He's always illegible!"

"So take away his pencil. You, instead, write for him," Tschisch suggested.

For some reason that horrified the girl. Her eyes bulged like moons. Separating her lips into weirdly opposed tides.

The boy wobbled. "It's no use. None of us will make it. Ah," he gurgled. "Who can write anyhow? Nobody survives!" Knocking over the stiff girl as he plummeted. Their two bodies crossed each other on the pavement like broken scissors.

But Tschisch didn't seem to mind. As if they were merely his coins to squander in the gutter. Spilled buckets. Litter.

Slitting the boy's cuff with a razor blade, Tschisch pocketed the evidence as his cat, scarred and fat, struggled toward him. Not to seem inadequate to his two-patient task, the Doktor shared his diagnosis. "Overdose of nutmeg!"

Rearing like a dolphin the cat embraced Tschisch. Then both of them crawled over the victims, licking their faces until they woke screaming.

"See, kids, no story is disaster," Tschisch said, while the opera of his patients tore their throats. "Other life always turns up. When I was your age I fought with my rival sex theoretician, Otto Weininger. That afternoon— October 4, 1903—did I hang myself? *He* did! Six years

later in summer I visited Professor Gumplowicz at
University of Graz. To challenge his sociology post! I
could disprove his notion that enemies are always outdoors. By the close of my visit, Glumplowicz and his
Wife fulfilled my thesis. *They suicided together*! That
ended our rivalry. I left them alone. But in my hands was
a page from his final manuscript. Now, kids, isn't it time
to submit that souvenir over to you, as my wedding
present?''

The girl and boy screamed louder.

Not bothering to muffle them, knowing nobody
would be disturbed on that block, Tschisch, the man of
perfect instinct, simply pivoted toward his third-story
room, saying, "That's it! That's what the boy was doing
up his sleeve. Proposing!"

The girl was immediately mesmerized into the Doktor's wake.

"To me?"

Thinking he also was heading in the Doktor's
direction, the boy lunged backwards. "That's not
what!" Then, startled by what he did not say, his mind
began dreaming again.

The girl yanked him as if he were her smashed-up
kite.

"No tricks! Admit what you wrote!"

Midway

up his dirty stairs Doktor Tschisch heard God congratulating him again. "What's your secret?" asked God.
Imagining himself a Hero to be reckoned with, reunited
now with his peach-pit munching sister, Tschisch felt he
could bargain for his best reward. "If you let my sister
and me become your official nose of mercy, I'll
divulge!"

An Angel intervened. "Are you suggesting that God
has more than one nose?"

Secure, Tschisch heard himself deserve the Holy
esteem. "From my Father I learned about God. Or,
actually, from one of his patients who wanted a second
nose sewn on his face. My Father asked him why. That
patient explained. According to his mystical tradition
God owned a nose of anger and a nose of mercy.

Whereas man, no longer in God's image, had thrown away everything except anger. No mystic, my Father refused. They fought. The patient claimed that God's original world hung in the balance. 'Correct me, correct Creation!' That's when I punctured the room, a four-year-old but full-time student of my own preoccupations. Announcing, 'Papa, I have two noses!' 'Out!' screamed my Father. 'Don't interrupt appointments!' Lifting my nostrils up, I insisted, 'No, look, I have two!' "

The Angel sighed from admiration. Tschisch, more at home now than he had ever been, and more the child, hallucinating all Heaven as his classroom and God his best pupil, pursued his topic with an arm around his sister's buttocks.

"How did an orphan like me succeed as physician to their broken love? Simply. Listen, to learn anything we must hold some funnel over our heads! That means— *repetition.* In other words, all understanding amounts at first to faith! Then comes rejection and argument. Allowing greater growth. Those who remain too long in initial category achieve just stickiness, an immunology that harms the self. Others, if too critical, if too enamored of their own voice, learn stubbornness, the curse of sterility. Where to open, where close, when to receive, when challenge. That's the single mystery I imparted. After my last lesson, I died. On schedule. If you want, test them now yourself, my kids. They know their stuff. I taught them everything. I was the sacred source they tapped like children. I was their Doktor

Viktor. I swear it, just as this girl here, my sister, was my only beloved, so my patients can spill over now and kiss like flames that lose no illumination by sharing. Some trick! The cup that runs over is never empty. Clear? Wasn't I ambitious for the world's good? Can you contradict me? Then hold me over your head like a funnel. Repeat after me!"

God Almighty was impressed. "It's only fair that I divulge a secret too. I miscast the universe with *my* two lovers. Adam and Eve! All the time calling me over to point out the obvious. A dog, a cat, a tree, a snake. Whatever they had to say was no news to me. Sick and tired of them around, I kicked them out. That's the real story. They bored me to tears!"

"I know that," Tschisch imagined himself say. "Can you tell me anything else?"

God said, "Did you ever hear of the wager I made with a wiseguy like you?"

Tschisch, at his door, waited.

God said, "He bet me he could prove that my world stunk! We drew up a contract. If after one day he did not see any child help another, eternal life was his. My equal! The moment we signed he laughed. 'Look at my face,' he said. 'I'm blind! Thank God! I won. Our contract says one thing, my face another. I'll never spy your goodness!' 'Let's make a second contract,' I asked. 'Where it reads *see*, insert *hear*! 'Okay,' said he. But once that correction was intrenched, he shoved his thumbs into his ears. 'Satisfied?' he yelled, though he couldn't hear his own voice anymore. 'Again, before our game commences, I'm winner!' I made a sad face, indicating that I'd like a third chance. He was prepared. He flashed me a final contract. 'Cannot hear or see,' said he. 'But I still can imagine. Let that become our agreement. Even on those terms, the terms of imagination which no man can control, I am certain of triumph. If I imagine any child doing a favor, I'm sunk. Take me off. If not, I exist on and on, like you!' I kissed his blank ears and eyes, to show that I harbored no hate. Any act of imagination, by day, by night, awake or asleep, and he had it, poor man. 'Hah,' celebrated the giddy freak. 'I might have won blind. Could have won deaf. But to be fair as He is foul, I chose imagination!' And he collapsed, once and for all!''

Anxious to return to his own lovers, yet wanting to be polite, Doktor Tschisch asked, "Where is he now? In the vicinity? Can I see him?"

"Certainly," said God. "He's still alive. Always shall be. But completely comatose. He outwitted me!''

In

actuality Tschisch hadn't fooled anybody. Both girl and boy were barking now like dogs against the Doktor's manipulation. The walk had not exhausted them. Tschisch's text of love, the cloth snippet fresh from the boy's pajama, was unacceptable. As far as they were concerned, Doktor Tschisch's heart could snap but they would not be carried from one idea to another like infants to their chambers. They refused to cooperate. The boy howled, "Liar liar!" So Tschisch again recited his scrap of evidence.

"Look what it says. *Marry me for a day. Marry me for an hour. Marry me anyway. Sweet, pickled, sour!*"

"That's no proposal," cawed the girl. "Don't match us like cracked plates. That's a suicide note. Stuff it, kid!"

Tschisch said, "I still say you're lovers."

The boy blanched, "Know what's wrong with you? You're always mouthing the same thing. You're a paraphrastic!"

"Thanks," said Tschisch. "On a child does it look bad?"

"Bad?" the girl screamed. "Did you drag him off the street for me? I have my life. Do you care? When I limber up, you can't tell where I'm heading. You have no key to my dance. Am I your asylum girl? I can protect my own name. I didn't come here dead! Keep hypnosis for yourself. I camouflage myself. So? Not always what's hidden sinful! I'm here because I'm Chinese. I can prove it. My eyes saw plenty of Hangchow boys with their trousers open in back for making. I'm nobody's slave. Want coffee? Do it yourself. Squash your cat's balls. *Sacrifice him!*"

As though no other choice were possible, Doktor Tschisch called over his cat. Kissing him on all sides, tail, belly, face. Afterward he chopped him under the throat until the animal gawked.

Tschisch's patients were more suspicious than surprised.

With a look of contrition so large it drawfed him, the Doktor suddenly knelt for his cat's forgiveness. Introducing a cellophane sack squirming with raw livers. But the instant the animal sunk his wide-eyed face into the small trough to get at the ovals of food, Tschisch plunged his hands into the cat's mouth, canceling the cat's reward. Now the cat's one ear dropped flat. The other, a gap in it as if drilled there as Biblical mark of servitude, swivelled loosely. Tschisch caught the cat with his hands and knees, pinning him. Then, as best he could, started urinating on him.

The drenched cat somersaulted free, spiraling bizarrely, smashed each wall like a demolition weight, and collapsed in a corner, crouching, unhinged. Whereupon Tschisch, like a lecturer, made his point.

"Kids, that's what happens when somebody you love treats you as shit. And that's what you two look like."

The girl yawned, "His cat's trained. "It's a circus act!"

"You've wasted your cat," the boy said.

Doktor Tschisch now wept.

"Don't make my mistake! Never postpone passion. When I was six was time to love my sister. *Before mumps*! To save her life. Don't be squeamish. If any mouth foams—result of damaged heart—breathe into it! But as boy I shied off. My information kept for myself. When she fantasized wrong on sex I let her. She couldn't appreciate what an erection was. Except once! Mending my knickers she saw me. I explained, 'Can't enter needle unless thread be stiff!' Her fingers she stuck up my nose and laughed. *I failed her*! Can't it be amended now?"

"Not after your freak slandered me on his pajamas. Not after you pissed on your cat!"

As the girl exercised, Tschisch's cat wobbled backwards toward the window as though he had forgot how to move, and jumped out.

The Doktor didn't even motion goodbye. "Let's

negotiate," he sobbed. "*You* won't dance, *he* won't scribble and *I'll* drop medicine! Agree? Just love? I'm anxious to put my autopsy in your hands! Obituary too. Right now!"

Swinging off his mattress the boy stooped over the girl, flattened his mouth against her ear and puffed inaudibly, "Let's tie him up before he kills us. We belong in hospitals."

She had her answer to whisper: "Creep!"

Unable not to nag, the Doktor asked, "What he say? His sex's appetite out of control?"

"Nothing on myself," spouted the boy, almost certain now that she was Tschisch's accomplice. "My life doesn't hang open like some garbage truck. No fact, no legends, no rumors, no memories. I'm sick!"

The girl said, "Some lover!"

Tschisch advised, "So confine all your remarks to her!"

The boy asked, "Want my real opinion?"

"Shoot!" screeched the girl.

"Her life's over!"

On her back the girl said, "Sock him for me. He needs another coma."

Suddenly swept by an urge to joke, the boy jutted his face at her and said, "Wouldn't want a sock from you. Too dirty!"

Twice she belted him with both legs knocking him out. As the boy's back smacked the sheets, the Doktor hugged the girl, quieting her with a kiss up and down her neck.

"Love makes mistakes."

"I pity him if he ever wakes."

"That's love, to pity!"

"You can't know what it's like to have him around again."

"Now you remember him? Your man?"

"He's no man. A man would insist I love him."

Tschisch said, "You be man. Convert. Why frustrate him?"

"That's what he does to me," she cried. "I don't know the bum. But he bugs me! He's like rubbish I can't get rid of."

"Claptrap."

Doktor Tschisch gently lifted her onto the boy, then climbed himself above the girl. So they were a triple-decker now, with Tschisch and the girl face down, and the skinny boy at the bottom face up, as a kind of keel to the shaky ship.

"Forgive him," murmured Tschisch.

Without understanding why, she almost kissed his unconscious face. But the boy woke too soon.

"You're an idiot," she said.

"Get off me," the boy requested.

She spat into his hair.

In place of any storm, the Doktor crooned his own name. "Tschisch, tschisch, *tschiiiiiiiiiiiiiiisch*! How long was that?"

"One second."

"One hour," disagreed the boy.

"Compulsion versus hysteria. Me? I'm punctual. I know exactly when to die."

"When?" she asked.

"After you kids make out."

"Impossible," cried the boy, trying to squirm free.

Tschisch counterchanted, "Tomorrow you steam, like steps of wood in winter sun, wall-eyed from passion. Tomorrow Tigris meets Euphrates. Tomorrow, an accomplished man, I conk under!"

"It's a bet," chimed the girl.

"Count me out," pleaded the pinned boy, like a boxer to the referee to end the fight.

"What can she do without your big toe?"

"Have you sex on the brain?" murmured the boy. *"Your mind has mumps!"*

Increasing his leverage, one sneaker on the red linoleum, Tschisch confessed, "That's what they said in Berlin. You remind me of 1926, the International Congress for Sexual Research, and my filibuster on 'Sex and Bismarckian Politics.' After I covered sex for animals and leaders by Triple Alliance, Potential Axis and Cordial Entente, I was thrown out. As *persona with no diploma.* As junk."

"Exactly," the boy said.

"Actually, as Freudian troublemaker. Only two ducks of Doktor Freud attended. Me and Adler. Now, boy. Make *your* admission of love. On identical wind as hers.

Tell us your story. Where did you meet her? On a train?
In your pajamas?"

"I cannot," the boy gasped. "I'm dying."

"Life is one foot here, one there," burped Tschisch.
"Talk! We won't get off otherwise."

The boy's ginger eyes turned white. "Life is death."

"Talk again," said the Doktor.

"Never," claimed the boy.

"Anybody on my side?"

Baring half her looping bosom, the girl made an
ultimatum of her own.

"Talk, or I'll ball you!"

"What do you want from me? Are you his sister? Are
you playing some game on me? You can't trick me into
marrying you!"

"Keep it short," added Tschisch.

"But sexy," she said. "If it's good, we'll marry you."

The boy thought. Then ventured.

"Though

beautiful and twenty-two already, she did not know her legs had to open for sex to happen."

"That's what I mean," the girl said. "He's always shitting on me."

"Try another one," Tschisch said.

"I don't usually do love stories," explained the boy. "My work's philosophical. Eccentric. About blemished people. Neighborhood nitwits."

"Cut the crap," she said. "Start, or suck my nipple! I may be a dancer, but tits I got!"

"For foreigner she speaks English good," complimented Tschisch.

"The boy was eleven. The girl, fifteen and a half. Yet such good lovers that after one session, she was pregnant."

The girl rocked her right bosom.

Tschisch said, "Again!"

"Some jerk in New York boards my ship."

"Finally yakking about yourself, kid?" asked the girl.

"It's a story," the boy blurted. "Can't I pretend I'm an Israeli sailor with a red beard, bangs, tight pants cut at the knees, wild yet innocent?"

"Yes," the Doktor said. "But she asks why he comes aboard? Where's your ship pointed? Does it sink? Why call him jerk? What's your story about? Love?"

"Can I go on?"

"All right," the girl allowed.

"My jerk has one purpose. To reach Israel. Work his way there by sea. The crew asks, 'Hey, that all you can talk of? Where's cunt around here? You got some sister?"

"Sister?" said the Doktor.

"The jerk I take under wing."

"Is this your idea of romance?" the girl snarled.

"The jerk's love waits for him on some kibbutz! Better?"

The girl ordered, "Set sail!"

The Doktor said, "Give him room."

"Once we hit Israel the jerk's heart's on fire. First I show him half the country. Then his kibbutz. The jerk! I decide to teach him a lesson. His own girl wants me. One night I almost put it in her three bunk beds away from him. But she holds back. By dawn I'm a wreck. Later, in my Jerusalem flat, she phones to say she's coming after me. Another night. Another wreck. Nothing! Two months pass. Her again! This time to claim she is pregnant. How? She watches me panic and pack my bag. With no goodbyes I zoom off screaming to Haifa. Prepared to sign on any steamer. They say, 'Jerk! A telegram you got from us? You're here? There's no ship!' Maybe one will show up? I hang around. I despair. They say, 'Jerk! Hurry. You have two minutes. Dock five!'

"I make it. In the engine room bumping into an army chum, I ask, 'Where we heading anyway?' My pal burps, 'Don't you know? It's a tramp. Five year deal. Far East!' Three whole days I sob. Motor man in stupor. My life all ruined. After months of boiler room noise, endless drink and talk about cunt, I am calm again. My friend pronounces, 'Just so many fucking hours. If you don't fill them or if you make slip-ups, your end is terrible. That's what they check on in the world to come. It's all there. In a book. Your fucking record!'

"Israel to New Orleans. New Orleans to Japan. Where somehow that girl's letters reach me. Her Hebrew ornate. She may be ugly, but a head she has! Not bad. I answer her. I'm the only sailor with a correspondence."

"I'm not interested in your mail," the girl said. "What happens in Japan?"

"At Kobe the crew is delirious. *Out of the way! Where are the cunts?* We march at night, the whole group, to a cabaret. If thirty thousand whores operate in town, we want them all! For a bottle of scotch and the teenage girl that accompanies it, I pay twelve bucks. Me and my whore! I drink for both of us. But at the end the barkeeper won't let her come with me. Murder enters my eyes. I sweep dozens of glasses off my table, lift the creep up, then think. Japanese cops are brutal. Incredible nation, so polite, so cruel. 'Shit, forget it, I won't force her!' Everyone on ship has something except me. First night ashore! I'm whore-less!

"For consolation, I bang at my pal's cabin. Busy! And who is his whore? My girl from the cabaret! 'How did you get her here?' She hides under a pillow. My friend says, 'By phone! I doubled the price of some jerk who already paid for her!' 'That jerk was me!' Exit the jerk. My friend comes downstairs after me, naked. 'Here, you fuck her!' After a moment he throws her in and shuts my door. Nobody forces *me*! I'm *reading*! The girl starts knitting. That bitch! I turn three pages and say, 'Shower!' She stands. 'No like me? I go.' We struggle at the shower. Me shoving her in, she pushing back out. 'No! I away!' My buddy's head reappears. 'Cut the noise, start fucking!'

"Now we're locked in. She holds my face, massaging me until I'm dizzy. A new person, I fuck her. Next day she washes and irons my every piece of clothes. I celebrate ashore with her. Earrings, coats, a red guitar. All for her. Every cent. She stays on with me though I'm broke and her *mamasan* shrieks for her."

"Her what?" the girl asked.

"Her *mamasan* is her owner," the boy explained. "Her father sold her to a bathhouse to pay for an operation on his back. *They* re-sold her to the *mamasan*."

Covering her bosom the girl cried.

"You can stop there," said Tschisch.

"If he does I'll kill him," said the girl.

Still the lowest member of the pile, the boy continued.

"After my morning shift, she's gone. Where? Back to her *mamasan*? What about our new love? I borrow five hundred and fifty bucks from my Captain. I storm her cabaret. An American sailor has her. She conceals herself behind a curtain. Her *mamasan* lets me purchase half of her from him with my Captain's dough. But before I can round up the remainder, my tramp sets out for Africa. That five year shuttle! Okay. Let her whore till I'm back to marry her."

"How do you know what she'll do?" barked the girl.

"At least it ends in a marriage," Tschisch said.

The boy said, "But at the Congo I need a woman again."

"You're the whore," said the girl.

"We're on anchor, lying in international waters as the Congo flames with revolution and me with passion. By Captain's command, nobody can leave ship. However, a black man taunts the crew from a small boat, promising us Africa's softest piece. At midnight I descend the hurricane rope. In the bush mosquitoes sting, leeches pinch, my clothes aren't clothes anymore. My destination turns out—an old lady sprawled in dead leaves and shit. With goats everywhere, I slap it in. He accompanies me back, for his fee. I'm already midway up the rope when he bangs the hull. Spinning in the dark. My Captain doesn't wake. And I don't pay!"

"Asshole!" the girl said.

"Later comes another chance. In Angola amid more fighting Africans. This time *I* do the urging. 'It's a ghost town down there! Paradise for the asking! Let's grab!' My buddies are not interested. Alone I land. The image of my Japanese whore frenzies me. I steal an old Buick, drive to the Capital drunk, United Nations police stop me and threaten to jail me. I run into a field and, alongside a hotel that looks defunct, I munch my favorite meal. Raw corn. A black bell-hop watches. From his wrist to his shoulder climb military stripes. Sergeant's mainly. After a while he arrests me. 'Why you to take my corn? It be my country. You to kill Jesus? You to be Jew?' I keep eating. 'Jesus didn't pay taxes!' 'Why you to say that?' 'He didn't!' 'Jesus honest!'

Tschisch interrupted.

"We're waiting for the wedding!"

The boy accommodated.

"Back in Kobe I'm promoted to donkey man, cancel all my debts, establish a house and citizenship in Hong Kong. And, at last, now own the whole whore! But I can't marry her. She annoys me. She has no will of her own. All she cares about is for me to be comfortable. Even if it means my stepping on her feet. Who can live with her? If I offer her a beer, 'No thank,' she says. If I insist, she accepts. Outside she faints at the gutter. Rain streams over her, passers-by only look, I raise her in my arms. I'm in a foreign land. What can I understand about Japanese? My tiny woman is dead! What killed her? I'm caught by horror. My friend slaps her face, washes her head. She wakes. 'Can't drink beer,' she says."

"A nice girl you married," said Tschisch.

"Not yet! We are re-routed to Havana. My ex-whore shares house with another ex-whore, my Captain's sweetheart. But I forget her in Cuba. I haunt bordelloes. My new Captain is an Hungarian with tattoes from his neck down to his prick, an advertisement for Crucified Jesus. One early day he rouses me to rescue Havana from Castro: 'Fuck Castro! He'll close up the whores!' I parade the wharf till noon. Havana lost, we sail for the States. There my buddies look to start another life. They force me to locate that American girl who wrote me superb letters. 'Run her Father's clothing business. Supply the army with uniforms. Divorce her. Split up the millions with us!' If I can't have my Japanese whore, why not learn from their lecture! They're a group. I'm one. Sacrifice. That's the only way to make good!"

"Fool," the girl said.

"The girl's address is Berkeley. They haul a barber to me. Shaved, spic and span in my Hong Kong wedding suit, I'm on my first plane of my life. In the air the motor no longer rumbles. Guilty, I gaze around. Everyone is relaxed. Are Americans cruel too? Where's the pilot's announcement? The engine is dead! A tall stewardess asks me to remove my shoes. What for? My socks stink! 'Slippers? A drink?' Reciting a list I don't recognize. I ask for whiskey. 'On the rocks?' 'Rocks? Rocks?' I am a worse dumbbell than any Japanese bride.

"In California nobody greets me. I collapse. For two days I haven't slept. I'm waked by a slob in shorts and sneakers who says, 'I don't recognize you!' In her Corvette I slip back to sleep. She hits me. 'Wake up!' At her stucco estate they offer me coffee. It trembles in my palms. 'Are you sick?' her Mother asks. I drowse. 'Off to school,' says my girl. 'Meet everyone!' That night at the dinner table her Grandad can't stop talking. 'Bullshit,' I intrude, and yawn as the whole family gawks. 'What's wrong? Can't I say *bullshit*?' Her Father taps my shoulder. 'Son, our daughter loves you. That's enough for us!' I stare at him. 'Son, she didn't write those letters to you. *I* did!' I rise, stumble outdoors, wire my ship for a ticket and sail back to the Far East."

Tschisch sighed.

"My ex-Captain and his whore are at the Hong Kong docks. 'Your house burned today to the ground. We can't find her. She's not around anywhere!' We scour the city. I'm already berserk. The sun sinks. My former Captain hugs me. 'The fire was three days ago,' he says. 'There wasn't enough of her for a funeral. She's no longer yours. Marry someone else!' "

"Bullshit," the girl said and punched the window, cracking the glass open. "You'll marry nobody!"

Then

as if she were air swung herself out.

Face cocked at the ruined window, the boy witnessed her flash downward faster than any beanstalk Jack, her finger-joints smeared with whitish dust, the remains of last summer's aphids. After a few moments, it was too much for him. He passed out on the floor.

Not yet alarmed, Doktor Tschisch planned to overtake her in his arms, he as farmer, she as fallen fruit. But by the time he managed his stairs to re-enter the scene, she was gone.

His

mind pickling, the Doktor carried the boy downstairs, re-strapped him inside the wagon, then circled around in quest of the girl, trundling his numbed feet like smashed propellers. One chrome button of a pedal sparkled despite its rust.

Quick maneuvering was impossible. Trash mounds saddled sidewalks, ready for tomorrow's collection or the End of Days. Besides, the Doktor was now exhausted. If only he could leave the boy behind! But he couldn't. Alone in the room he might mimic his partner, climb out, land on his head. Without the boy, the girl meant nothing. Yet without *her*, why keep *him* anymore? Half miracle was no miracle.

He whirred more backwards than forwards. Hour by gloomy hour. Non-stop, except to invade a hole, scrounge on all fours under a porch. At five in the morning Tschisch admitted that he had reached the vanishing point.

But in a sudden burst of guesswork the Doktor struck for the open road full-speed, whacking parked cars on either side, as if his goal were to fracture himself. Like a sacrificial Isaac, the boy made no complaint. Nor did the Doktor once look back to check his passenger's comfort or safety. The boy lay back, as if torpedoed there.

Finally Tschisch's tricycle came to rest, at a spot that looked like Hell. A mangy field fronting the girl's former asylum. She'd have to be crazy to be back here, but Tschisch had no other choice, no other idea. He parked his complicated vehicle, lugged the boy on his back like a laundry bundle, and stumbled in.

Behind the door three women welcomed him with spittle. The Doktor regurgitated a soy bean. Munched it again for energy. Could he hint about the missing girl, expose his trespass yet achieve straight facts? Did they recognize him as her kidnapper?

"Full," said the smallest lady. "Get out!"

Half unconscious himself, Tschisch fell into the mens room, where a rancid voice behind a stall said, "Where's your stick?"

The Doktor speculated no longer. His mind was made up.

Out, racing against dawn, furious, at the end of his life, Tschisch barged into another hospital. Its waiting room was stuffed. Tschisch adjusted the boy into the last wheelchair like a doll. Patients were bleeding, moaning, hailing physicians but with no luck, pointing to gouges or fractures, interested in only their own pain. Tschisch spent a few depleted moments arranging the boy's expression, then kissed his each eye, wobbled to the main counter, signed a paper as if he were the victim asking immediate care, submitted it to the small-nosed nurse, identifying for her the boy slumped against the side wall in the last row, and exited, not knowing where he was bound, following his tricycle's lead.

Anyway, the Doktor could not have recognized the girl if he had found her.

She'd costumed herself in castaways. Purses hung from her neck like breasts, numberless layers of rags and knotted towels ballooned across her shape more ominously than Medusa's heads. Her face was trestled by two pairs of smashed spectacles. Earth did not look civilized enough for her. Yet, despite her preposterous get-up she seemed at home in herself, complete, disinfected, in obedience only to her own eyes for everything from law to decorum. In fact, she appeared sane. If in minutes flat she'd pieced together an outfit, why couldn't she herself be salvaged?

But even now she saw the world back off from her. She was just a burden, a fish from water. They'd agree with her tormentors. First she must admit she was insane.

Like Hell she was! Her problem was that she was

another nation's handiwork. Her mannerism confused everybody. Like the Sikh she noticed an hour ago yawning on the corner, his turban a blue coconut. Sweetly his delicate hand fluttered across his lips to decorate his yawn. She, a Chinese junk ship with rusty hair, adored his art, his morality. It was her way of yawning too.

But it was good to walk by herself again. No longer kept on the wrong side of the table, out of reach of her own life. Rather than remain a customer in an empty store, she'd curl with dead cats as rubbish.

Could she endure another pornographic smack to her face? Two men in her room? A fake Doctor and fake lover! If she hadn't escaped they would have bilked her brain. Tricked her into eating from a hat. All minds were tragic. The machine wanted meaning so badly it took poison. Any substitute was allowed. Even a freak was worth affection!

For example, no matter where or how often she escaped, her conclusion was another asylum. Always came confinement. First they told you to open, then punished you for anything you did. Ordered you sing, afterward made fun of your voice. Not that her asylum days were wasted. She learned life's lesson—*someone was always worse than you*! Like that bald girl who shared a room with her Mother, who'd already spent thirty poker-faced years there. Everyone knew her story, how the bald kid, before she went nuts, was reared by a male two-some, her Dad posing as Uncle, her Uncle posturing as Dad. They refused to explain their masquerade after the girl caught on, so she fell under the identical lock and key as her heavily made-up Ma. Life obviously was a system to keep suicidals alive as long as possible. She herself dreamed every night of doing herself in. When her turn would come, others could suck their comfort from her.

She had trekked around enough. Why was there no bed for her in the railroad station? What was the good of amassing her costume with pouches galore for travel convenience? She hoisted herself up several trees, hand stood, exercised inside a telephone booth, suspended there for hours, back and feet to either wall, enjoying herself. As long as nobody asked for sex and no Doctor told her to fuck all he wanted and she didn't have to hear whore stories she was a happy kid.

But her situation was still dangerous. Her new Doctor was a child. He might discover her secret. In fact, by way of absolute precaution, while he or the boy were around, she tried not to remember it herself. Her mind was sore from such restraint. But that kid was worse. He'd stay nuts anywhere. Even America. He was in touch with nothing. Whereas she? Let a horse and buggy pass her, she'd catch the message under the cart, spelled by the horse's four legs in Chinese. Only she!

Maybe Tschisch was right? Why couldn't they, she and the boy, share a bed or words? His argument from allergy made sense. Prior contact? Was that stubborn boy involved in her secret? Was he part of the trap which, three years ago, fooled her innocence, making her a target for pornography?

They took her to a room where she imagined herself finally free, done with false adoption and caretaking, away from homes and asylums, in the arms of her own talent, appreciated for what she was, a unique dancer, her eyes wilder than pirouetting legs. As she bounded from window to table naked, cameras clicked under the floor. They made her a bum. She was in everybody's hands. Any eye could gaze at her madness. How could she now save her name?

Offer herself to some college as a model star for opera or harp? Could she reminisce about China or bump again into Mao Tse Tung? Organize America around her flag, adopt all insane as her wards, shower with them, feed them, read to them? Would America allow her now such freedom?

Unwinding all her garbs as though nothing were needed for her final answer, the girl danced.

The frantic Doktor, having signed his boy in as Viktor Tschisch, found himself collapsed on his own stairs. As he fell into bed a voice said, "Finally? It's you I'm after. I'd do anything for us now."

Over the covers lay the naked girl.

Stunned, Tschisch had balance enough to say, "Wait a little longer." Then kissed her mouth, buffed her pudenda, scrubbed her bosom and exited.

Exploiting his luck, Doktor Tschisch hurried to City Hospital, catching the boy in his arms, and transported him to his quarters again, thanking God for a second chance at Paradise.

Part Three

The

Doktor celebrated the best way he knew. With ropes. Buttressing their intimacy until his patients could only move in unison.

"I'll be right back," Tschisch said and locked the couple in his room. Ear to door, anticipating ultimate fireworks, Tschisch waited in the hall.

The girl, handicapped, rampaged. The boy spun in her tight company, watching her from half pity, half horror. She had another crack at the window, smashed the backs off two wicker chairs, and pulled apart each text upholding the cursed bed.

"What's wrong with you?" asked the boy, his mouth by necessity entering hers. "You crazy?"

As if consisting of a thousand separate birds she swirled across his vision, throwing at him her own orders.

83

"Don't talk! Crook! *You stole my story!*"
The boy was tongue-tied.
"Remember the day we met? I shocked you. I was your Japanese whore. Kiss me, creep!"
"That isn't so," the boy managed.
"You'll love me the rest of your life. Stuck to me forever, leper!"
"I couldn't for one day," the boy sagged, taking the girl with him.
Behind the warped door Doktor Tschisch, at that point, had to participate. "Don't exaggerate! Your type, kid, could live with a roach!"
Not aware where that voice came from, the girl froze. Though her life was always subject to intrusion, she refused to be treated like a gangplank to some unseen schooner.
The boy also was woozy. He wanted to scream for help. Yet could not open his mouth.
The Doktor listened for a while to nothing. Then he couldn't waste any more time. He barged in.
"Did I miss it? You made out?"
No reply.
"Wasn't she satisfied?" Tschisch asked, surveying now the damage. "Hey," shaking the boy's legs. "She wrenched everything except you. Understand? She showed you her love. Will you marry her?"
The boy moaned, "Stop that."
"Why?"
"Can't you see? We're wrong for each other."
"Not if you pick up where you left."

"Can't argue anymore. I'm dying, it's finished."

Was that his last moment the boy wondered, was he vanishing, was it the instant of his passage to death?

"Doesn't your mind want another chance?" asked Tschisch. "Why have the same mistake?"

As if by cue the girl woke. "He's looking for somebody smarter than him. That can't be. His mind weighs a ton! Lead!"

Now the boy blackened, his last word very practical, "*Ambulance!*"

"Congratulations!" laughed Tschisch, almost swallowing his tongue. "You caught him!"

The girl snapped, "Want another tragedy?" crawling beneath Tschisch's broken books like a sea monster under a wall, with the boy thinking he was on the road to his hospital. "Idiot," her concealed voice continued. "You won't squeeze anything more from us."

Tschisch answered, "There's time. Both of you sleep. Meanwhile I fix your wedding shoes."

Sucking half his fingers the Doktor piped as addendum, "All stories are borrowed. Don't be angry at your boy. Didn't you yourself learn of that Japanese whore by one of your sailor guardians? Dream life more with compassion than clarity. End your captivity. It's the right moment. Prepare for it!"

Later

the girl's harrowing whisper stoked the dead of day.

"Was your Father's sister crippled?"

Tschisch was tempted to throw his voice again into the match, answering for the unconscious boy. Instead he waited.

"Did her head almost hit the sidewalk as she rocked? Did she tout life on any terms? Brush her silver hair outdoors, as though she owned what all her neighborhood wanted? Was she a great woman?"

Her question came at an odd time. The boy lay dreaming now, become his own Father, growing up all over again, except this time with a sister so lame and so deaf that he could no longer devote his life to himself. Perhaps her question had actually initiated the boy's dream. In any case, he was unwilling to part from his lost situation. Since he had never inquired of his Father what possessing an impaired sister was like, the boy now imagined himself doomed underground, doomed to explore the secret consciousness of his dead Father. How could the boy survive otherwise? In spite of their intense involvement, they had hardly spoken to each other, fearful of any breach, any argument, any shame.

"Was your family stuck with a passionate cripple?"

Dredged to the surface, the mystified boy spoke, seeking a face in the damaged ceiling. "My Father's sister. I think so. I remember. Somebody said it. I guessed it."

The boy had finally admitted something.

"I met her," the girl said.

"How?"

"On her day of death."

"Whose?"

"My hair she kissed for comforting her."

As though himself again, the boy decided, "Coincidence! That lady's head was dark. Clearly now. I recall. Not silver!"

Scrutinizing her palms like a script the girl asked, "And me?"

Under too much pressure, he slumped into sudden inoperativeness.

"Not worth remembering?"

Except for an asymmetrical flutter of his eyelids the boy contributed nothing on that subject. He was busy making an addition in his mind to his own possible biography. Was he the boy who had been schooled in

Catholic establishments though he was Jewish, who ran away to Italy in protest, masquerading as priest, collecting an enormous batch of evidence against the Church, through confessions in every village, from other priests, in order to disclose a world conspiracy of gangsters, but on his way back he was beaten in some Central American garage, his trunk of documents burnt to ashes, concluding all his activism?

"You don't like my conversation?" asked the girl. "I deserve a man of wisdom," she explained squatting now on her hair. "With more time, I can improve my speeches," forcing the boy's mouth open with her thumbs, "I can rehearse!"

The boy howled.

"Don't do that," screamed the girl and seized his tongue.

It slipped from her fingers.

"You—sound—familiar," enunciated the boy slowly. "What?"

Her gawk half mimicked love.

The boy said, "In a story of mine, some character always is rehearsing. To copy his hero, Hitler!"

"Ah," sighed the girl in disgust. "That's you. My genius! Turning whatever I say to the worst. Always assigning me every fault in history. You never allowed me my own vision. You raped me! For that you're going to lose me, kid. I hate you now more than ever. Fool!"

Like an innocent child, the boy asked, "Who are you?"

Tired of breaking from her stupor only to compile strings of rebuffs, insults, confusions, misentanglements, failures, the sour girl, over-disappointed, sick of her entire story, she hauled herself and the boy and the Doktor's giant dracaena to the window, shoved its bulk far out into the half-bleached indecisive air, hoisting the enormous flower pot itself above the level of the sill until tree together with its heavy cylinder of earth shot downward in a near silent act of suicide. Afterward the girl squirmed into the pot somehow, making a triangle of herself and the boy, imagining them both a parcel to be shipped to Hell at the cheapest rate.

"What does that prove?" asked the boy.

"That she wants to grow!" intervened Tschisch. "Nitwit, it's happening before your nose. Stay with her. Don't drift our subject. Your fiction's one thing, she another. Without her you're zero. Stubborn kid! Now my dracaena suffered from you. That tree measured my American visit, twenty-seven years my best patient, high as my ceiling and sideways her face showered me, flowering indoors miraculous, my many-handed goddess with her own idea how to stay lovely. I ordain you to replace my tree. Take your girl and bloom indoors!"

"You can't do this to people," gasped the boy, his hands as dazed as his head. "Can't trick them of their own lives. Can't prey on their confusions. That's murder!"

"You suspect me still?" said the Doktor. "Of what? Wasting my last three days in America hunting for snapshots of former patients, that Viennese couple from *Krankenhaus*? I wedded them long ago. They reside in a mirror now of their own love, somewhere inside that very hospital as in a ship. What's fishy in this room here? Your facts you know now. Quick as a prisoner making your escape, veer to her arms!"

"You're a liar!"

"So what?" said Tschisch, biting off two nails. "Even if all liars were Greek and me Greek, trust me. Can I lie *all* the time?"

"You must be her last relative," said the boy, his face washed with sweat.

"What, according to you, is love?" demanded the Doktor, following his own logic.

"Maybe you're hired to marry her off," muttered the boy.

"Say for once what is love!"

"Taking for granted," blurted the boy, uncertain whether he had said what he meant to, or the opposite.

"That's why she's yours forever," agreed the Doktor. "You took her for given."

"I cannot talk with you anymore."

"My tongue hurts too!"

"We have nothing in common. Whatever you bless, I curse."

"Explain," requested Tschisch. "I can learn from a twenty-year-old."

"Love lasts only when it has something else accompanying it."

"What?"

"Reason!"

"That's a rope for hanging. Passion has no reason. No matter who with. Who without!"

"No value to the choice," recited the boy, "no value to the chooser."

"Only the Devil can't find somebody to love."

"I'm human," pleaded the boy. "I cannot love by accident."

"How else does God love?" said the Doktor. "Yet what's man worth?"

"Man's better without God's love," screamed the boy, as though he were sighting a whale.

"For your sake," wept Tschisch, "don't throw my last lesson away."

"You're wasting your time," said the boy.

"Aren't you lonely without her?"

"I'm sorry for her. But she's not mine. I'm sick. I'm losing my eyes again," the boy's one arm limp, the other afloat sailing by his face. "Again. You're the lonely one. *You* marry her. I won't pull through. This is it. Get me my pencil."

Kissing the boy across his mouth Tschisch urged, "I'll marry you then instead!"

"I accept on one condition," said the girl, not interrupting her complicated posture or facing anybody. "No children!"

As

though reconciled after a storm, the three of them watched the last set of sun from their common refuge, Tschisch's cock-eyed bed.

"Could you leave us alone?" the boy asked. "Maybe we two would recognize each other."

"Absolutely," said Tschisch.

"But this time don't stick your ear in," the girl said.

"What do I need ears anymore for?" said Tschisch. "You want to deafen me? I'm ready."

The door locked. Silence burned the room.

The girl and boy, not knowing why they were still sharing a bed, stared at each other.

"Are you really from China?" asked the boy.

"Are you from Argentina?" the girl answered.

"Do you know what's happening here? Actually? For what purpose are we together?"

"It's where we belong," the girl said. "The last room, the final experiment. If we fail, they chop our legs so we can't run off. Something like that. What are you in for, kid?"

"I don't understand."

"Leprosy? Faulty wiring? Old age?"

"Do you know that man?" asked the boy.

"The sex maniac?" she said. "We've seen him before. We heard his story! He's sick himself. Mumps. Who you anyway?"

"Me?" said the boy, relapsing into his dream of self-scrutiny.

He had not heard all of the Doktor's orations, but he'd soaked enough to decode that he and the girl were somehow a continuation of the Doktor's life. To replace Tschisch and his sisters. Why? Because like Tschisch and those three or four sisters, he and the girl were broken. It made sense. Everything ends. Life must follow death. But Tschisch didn't want perfect creatures to stand where invalids once sat. The transformation had to proceed by degrees, not from garbage to manna, not from blemish to total joy. Only victims could do the trick, two persons whose minds were practically shut off. They now were the Doktor's dead skin, part of his circle. That's what the boy understood.

Was he mistaken? Were he and the girl not strangers? Should he be glad to commence his existence now from wherever the Doktor marked? Did he stand a chance of thinking directly, as though he were himself, focusing on any moment from his past, something as tiny as where he went to school, what had put him in a hospital? Did he have to restrict himself to the method of combing what he remembered of his fiction for details that clicked? What good was that? He recalled paying bums fifty cents for their lives, then being beaten up finally by one bum who returned to buy his story back after the boy had thrown it away, notes and all. Was that a story? It left him nowhere. Like the drunk's punches, it took no toll on him. Like watching his decrepit Aunt howl on the street after her ninety-year-old Father didn't wake that morning. Outdoors now her indoors. No cause now but hers. She plucked trees, cars, houses, the sky itself. Her ragman's cry, "It's all over. I'm an orphan now!" Duck-wobbling wildly, she knocked her head against the pavement. To the boy it looked as if she had stretched over a sea. As though her body burst. At the cemetery, she threw herself into the grave. The boy asked himself whether he would ever match such passion. Thereafter he judged himself by her standard. Only if he could catch up to her as she caught up to her dead Father, would he be fast enough for the act of love. Yet the memory of that woman, the cradle of his love, was probably more bogus than Tschisch's claim that the girl before him was his ultimate catch.

Anyway, the Doktor was already back. "Hey, what's wrong with him now? Did he confess his knowledge?"

"*Knowing is out*," said the girl. "He don't me, I don't him!"

"Where he collect his whore story?" complained Tschisch. "From you! You just admitted!"

"I lied, I got excited."

"Don't tease. Your boy told what he knows. He's waiting for you to stop pretending. See, he conked again."

"He's a liar like me. We never saw the rat before!"

The Doktor had another card.

"Okay," he said. "I'll say the truth. It's lousy. You are nearly strangers. You met once ago. On the street. You had an argument. Didn't agree for beans. Allergic, you hit each other. You wanted even murder. Instead parted instant enemies. So what? That came when he lost his Pa and you an asylum. You just were kicked from your home for unwed Mothers because you weren't pregnant. Why still be angry? No wonder in his hectic despair he tried to pick you. He done it to twenty others in three days since his Father's end. Naturally you rebuffed. He slandered back with 'What's you? Got lice up your ass?' That's nothing! My tradition says that there's no love without rebuke. You got on each other's nerves? Good. Now just thank me. I don't accept fees. It's a better story now. Recognize me? Elijah the Prophet! I come for nothing."

"You're the writer not him," she said. "His stories are all shell, no nut."

"Come celebrate. It's your second meeting with him."

"If this was our first time, I'd do it. But I know what he's like, forget it."

"All right," Tschisch sobbed. "*I'm* the liar! You caught me too. I made your whole love story up. Kiss the innocent boy now. *He's a total stranger!*"

"Not to me, I hate his guts. He'd rather walk his Father nowheres than accompany me for love. My rival. Let him marry his Father now. Do I care?"

Said Tschisch, "You don't know this boy. My heart, my heart."

"Am I here again?" asked the boy, plugging into the conversation suddenly.

"Quick," Tschisch said. "Tell her she can count on you from now on."

"Impossible," the boy said, thinking he was in another ambulance.

"Don't contradict," said Tschisch. "You just woke up. Why look for trouble? Impossible is for tragedy!"

"I won't kiss a comic," the girl said.

"So don't," barked Tschisch, banging his head on the wall as if he were a shoeshine boy attracting customers with his brush. "Instead wipe his ass. That's all I ask. Affection! Orphans, why chase away your life? See?" Hoisting her two arms. "Hairy! That comes from no sex. Her crotch spreads to three separate fires, but she still dances like a skeleton. Become world models. Let America make ballads of you kids. Manufacture yourselves fresh. Link your eyebrows, coo, be real citizens!"

"Why piddle with us?" the boy asked. "Offer yourself for world crises."

"I'm still an alien," the Doktor said. "I no got working papers. But actually, Presidents can learn from my method. God too."

The boy gasped, "I'm talking to myself, I'm ruining my mind. *You don't exist!*"

"What about me?" said the girl.

Working out his problem, the boy said slowly, "I invent him, he invents you. It's box within box!"

"I need none of you," she said, plunking a finger in her vagina. "I can dance under the table. You pukes will come out one day to congratulate me. I'm here for a headache."

Tschisch saw that his medical procedure had become untidy when both patients slumped into each other's arms unconscious.

"Your shoes," said the Doktor. "They prove no *vita sexualis*! He walks on toe tips, she on heels. Too cocky or cautious. Clamber up each other! A termite can't fell a redwood. A finch won't lopside any tree. And if you break, that's the crack of love!"

Boy and girl farted, but this time Tschisch was in no mood to join them.

"I'm going," he said, removing coat, sneakers, shirt. "I'm through."

One after another, Tschisch dropped his garments out his windowless window. Then picked up a mangled chair and angled it through, releasing it into the air.

"Knock my teeth out! Which is better? Death, jail, or love? I'm sick of you."

And Tschisch cut their ropes.

Sour,

unconciliated, the girl chose suffocation.

Everything was torment, including self-remembering. Ruts, not knowledge. Between past and present hung nothing but clothes lines. Self-hypnosis. China taught her two things. How to keep a secret and how to go to pieces when you least expected it. She could crack at dawn for no reason. She, the world's earliest mistress, kidnapped at age six, a nuisance placed on opium for three years, to keep her mum. No wonder she never awakened. Her strength, bravura and pretense. To conceal her virtual childhood, cover her non-growth, she labeled herself a loudmouth. But that was no release from madness. She lived in dread of exposing herself. Exposing herself as two children, real and adopted, a posed kid and repressed one, double-crossing herself always, robbing her contradiction of any dignity, her fear so endless it was fake, like all attempts to cure her, shaming her in public, making her sleep two weeks in a row, tugs of war, tugs of peace, nothing helped. Her mirror turned her inside out. It was time to exit.

Simultaneously the boy had an insight. Facts were not his salvation. He lived in another satchel. Ideas! If he wanted to find himself, he'd have to recall his old notions. Ancient Greece was lucky. Her idea was necessity. But the boy had chance. And when you worship chance, you worship God. His mind opened now. Seeing himself miniscule yet all-powerful, locked in a block of time with all mankind, the boy snoozed the longer and better.

Doktor Tschisch, however, was careful not to lose his wager in anybody's sleep. Presaging its third stain the sun lay slumping, warped from shape, amorphous.

"It's still booming," said Tschisch. "It's still distinct. That sun! See its human skull? Love, kids. Intense, up each other's wind!"

The boy at least stopped snoring, clearing one eye. But the girl was not in sight.

Nudging his patient by ear and shoulder Tschisch squeaked, "Where's your red partner?"

The boy's eye closed.

"Ah, she loves camouflage, an insect on a matching leaf, a seagull egg on beach among spotted rocks."

Like a customs agent the Doktor rummaged his room,

raking his torn texts, checking his laundry bag, the sink. Out the window. Had she escaped again? Shaking the boy like an orange-stuffed tree Tschisch howled, "Help me, boy! You're alive. I'm right. You're only sick from love. I'm the one who's dying!"

Crawling from under the rocked boy the suicidal girl shrieked, "You've spoiled my coffin!"

Tschisch sighed. "My Mother told me, always look under!"

"How come you're quoting her now?" she said.

Tschisch said, "A son can't talk much about his Mother!"

"Back to Hell!" she said.

Tschisch exited, "Break anything that's left. Enjoy each other. Lost and found in Dollarica! It makes my funeral. Goodbye. Just remember, always announce what you're worth. Eve didn't. She let Adam talk. But life's rule is if two approach one another, each claims to create the other. That includes God. The minute he confronted us, he gabbed first. Everything was his! That's how all ownership spreads, by word of mouth. Change that. I couldn't, you can. I'm dying, you're reborn. Come to your senses. You both existed before you met. And will after. Be man and woman, not magicians. Blame another, control another, create another, but always talk at the same time! The real secret's opposite of what you heard before. You don't need each other! *That's love*! Goodbye for good!"

With something like a bang, the Doktor vanished.

Recognizing the homicidal danger, both girl and boy

struggled to stay awake, she reminding herself to talk first, he trying to take Tschisch's other advice and squeeze her in his arms before any sun went out. But he couldn't touch her, and she couldn't speak.

Finally a peep from the boy as the girl accidentally flicked his knucklebone. "I hope," he said, "I'm not hopeless. I forget how to make love."

"I'm insulted," she said.

"Why?"

"It means I was lousy too! If we were lovers before!"

"But we weren't."

"How do you know?"

"Don't be a child."

"You know me?"

"Never!"

"Then he's right," she said. "That's what it comes to. You're too uncanny about me. I'm not sure now."

"What are you saying?"

"You ever compose a sentence about a swan?"

"Swan?"

"Squatting at the sea, hunting a more polished version of herself, fanning herself, private as a mirror. And so on. A long sentence!"

"That's close," said the boy. "A crane! Himself not herself. How did you know?"

"Kid, I made it up. You actually write that dumb?"

"Answer me!"

"I once was in love with a writer. It's contagious."

The boy smiled at her for the first time and sang, "*You're* the crook. I like you though."

"Really?" she said, posing. "What you see in me?"

All of a sudden the boy startled.

"What's wrong?" the girl asked, clapping his narrow face.

"I got frightened," he answered, sweating. "This bed's too small."

"Want to sit at the window? Fresh air?"

"Thanks," and accepted her assistance. "I can't know when fright will return," he admitted. "Squeak of a toilet handle sears me to the bone, as if I met my murderer."

"I thought you never talked about yourself."

"You're smart. Great memory."

"Thanks, that's what my friend used to say."

"Writers are alike."

Easing him down, she asked, "Woozy still?"

"It's gone," the boy said blinking at the fascinating sun. "How did you know I wasn't afraid of heights?" and leaned far out the window in a mock faint.

"I guessed."

"On what basis?" the boy laughed.

Smiling beaverishly, she shook her hair, refusing to release her secret.

"Your love?" joked the boy.

"You learn quickly," offering him a slight shove for reward.

Shifting to a more secure position along the ledge, the boy by mistake clouted his head against the frame and for a moment lost his balance. Immediately she caught the scruff of his neck, almost stumbling out the window herself.

"Why didn't you let me fall?" asked the boy. "You took a bad risk."

"You have to stick to someone in trouble."

All of a sudden the boy heard himself weeping, not now, before, in a scene with another girl, he couldn't recall who, but she was speaking her heart out, imploring him to stay with her, arguing her case like a lawyer, 'You can't abandon me as soon as you discover my darkness! If everybody did that nothing would hold. You must take my sorrow as yours. We are each other's burdens. We are!' When he opened his ears and mind again to what was circling in that room between him and the red-head, he found they were hugging. Backing off he asked, "How long have I been dreaming?"

"Not long," she said. "Look at what's left of the sun. Enough to make a day of! Want some tea? I had a friend—"

"I know, I know," interrupted the boy. "You're as bad as that quack. The two of you—paraphrastic!"

"Speak of the Devil," cried the girl pointing at the sidewalk below where Doktor Tschisch stood, head thrown back, making a series of signals toward his patients, pushing with both hands forward, directing his right thumb at the sky, laying his tilted cheek against his joined palms, all of which made clear sense to them, reminding them of the late hour, that it was time for them to dally in bed not at the window.

While she was preparing the tea, the boy eased himself back into bed, opening his pajama at the chest to expose his flesh. On her return the girl came lugging cup and kettle. At his bedside she hoisted the boiling water over his head asking, "Afraid?" The boy burst into sneezing and laughter.

"What's the matter?" she said. "I remind you of somebody now too? You think I wouldn't pour this stuff across your scalp, annoint you King of Casualties?" She angled the spout until the boy stopped laughing. "Answer me," she insisted. "Are you scared again?"

"I'm human," the boy said. "But it's inhuman of you to frighten me like this."

"My Mother made me brave. When I was nine she took me up in her airplane, showed me a parachute and said, 'Guess who jumps out now? *You!*' Come. If there's love, there must be song. Be mystic to me. Sing Chinese!"

The boy shut his mouth with one hand.

"This is only your first trial," she announced, wobbling the kettle as though she had palsy. "You'll cry like ten rubber toys when I'm through. Seduce me with your puny chest? I'm no ancient astronomer. Don't need your cave to calculate stars in! I'm me, I have a mouth big as an umbrella. *You're* the freak. You mute wind-bag! I'm a dragnet for you. Hate me but sing!"

"Would you get me a pencil and paper?" asked the boy.

"If you talk as you write. I can't read your scribbles. *Never could!*"

"Look," the boy shouted. "While I'm here, face facts. I don't know you!"

"That's why—always had your face in your fiction!"

"I pity you, you'll never have time to be yourself."

"Careful," she said, her kettle higher. "Want me to quote you? *Passion can be uprooted. Compassion never. Avoid compassion!*"

"You're getting me angry, I'll hit you, I swear it."

"A fight with blood on it, that's what we need to settle all differences. Then with clear conscience, we can love."

The boy's zags of tears stared at her.

"What wrong now?" she asked.

"You remind me of somebody."

"Someone you loved?"

"I think so."

"And you don't know me? You expect me to believe you loved some girl just like me, but not *me*?"

"I said you reminded me of her, not she was you or you her! Where's my pencil and paper?"

"Only if you write about us. Our ending."

"If you have—"

"Premonitions!" she said, as though her task were filling in blanks. "If you have premonitions like me, you should know how we end!"

"How did you know I was going to say that?"

"From the way you treat cats. You're always faced in the direction they come in. Do I get an ending?"

"In a dream."

"Whose?"

"Mine."

"A dream of what?" asked the girl.

"Dying."

"Mine?"

"Mine," answered the boy.

"You torture me."

"The other way," insisted the boy, buttoning his pajama. "He's downstairs, congratulating himself like a politician, while we, his broken country, go under. He wants to live like a man of high office—off our fears. We die."

"Make all of us live!"

"I can't."

"Then quit writing our story," she said.

"Okay. Can I have paper and pencil now?"

The girl poured him tea, stirring it with her thumb. "What you gonna compose, kid?"

"Don't worry. I'm rounding off a different story. Or beginning something new."

"I'm all ears."

After a pause the boy recited, "My hero is a man who won't be King. Who hides everywhere—inside a mattress, pot, harp, plough, asylum, the Holy Ark. Locates misfits to take his place, pours vinegar over his head to disqualify him, showing he can't rule even himself. You can scald him with your water, that's as good an ending as any!"

"And the other one?"

Gulping tea the boy said, "Starts with the seed of a betrayal. A Cranshaw pit."

The girl walloped the cup from his hand. "It began with a Persian mellon!"

"Watch it," the boy warned, trembling like the cursed leaf of Leviticus.   "You can't ask me to play dumb any more. I have eyes. My mind works now. I remember what I know!"

"Can you ask me to stay insane? Ask me to suicide? For what? One stone, one mistake?"

"I wasn't talking about you!"

"Don't give me that. I was the one, I'm the victim not you, I'm sick account of it. What are you crying about? If you don't love me, what's the difference if I wasn't faithful?"

"You're driving me crazy."

"That's love, kid," answered the girl, lifting the skirt of her nightgown. "The stupor I'm caught in. Can't do without you. But together's no answer either. We're in the same boat now. Serves you right."

"Please," the boy begged. "You don't have to pull any chair from under me. I'm on edge, my body, my mind, I can't even seat myself without landing on the floor. Leave me. Let me be."

"Isn't that what we said about you?" the girl asked. Chewing on her hem. "Remember? Said you were, the trouble far back, as a kid couldn't put ass on chair. They never checked for brain injury?" Showing her bosom.

"Does this room have peepholes? Or two-way mirrors? Is that what you two are up? Is he downstairs selling tickets? Are customers coming, to watch scenes of sex? Am I in some crazy European whorehouse?"

"Remember me now?" she asked, totally naked.

"Oh, my God!" the boy cried.

"Forgive me?" she said. "I'm here, you love me? So what if I poisoned your Father! I'm yours. Be my psychiatrist again! Enough stories. I want to live happy."

In

the nick of luck, the ordeal closed.

At the very flat tire of Tschisch's fortune, down to his final dollar. The last fruit of his Father's persistent practice from capital to town to village. But Tschisch was unworried. His valuables lay buried in the sunk ship of afterlife.

Downstairs on the pavement Tschisch lingered, enjoying the municipal flash and sway of life before climbing back up to die. Creation would soon be his toy no more. His infancy was over.

Apparently it was election night. A van announced to a crowd, through its faulty loudspeaker, "I'm for you. You're for me. How's that?"

Tschisch didn't wish to exit America on that suspect note. His ear caught two teenagers squatting on a curb. A boy and girl. They were discussing their sex lives.

The girl said, "I get it. You're cheating on her and don't think it's fair, so you want to break it up, right?"

The boy whistled.

She offered, "I'll tell her. What do I care if she thinks I'm one of the chicks you been balling. I ain't!"

The boy said, "Thanks. Can I do anything for you?"

The girl flashed her crooked teeth. "I'm in trouble. Cops after me. Three years ago I stole a car!"

The boy shoved her shoulder. "They can't touch you now. They got no witnesses. Three years, three years!" He added, "What else?"

The girl said, "How come I gotta pay alimony?"

The boy repeated, "Alimony? Not you! He pays that!"

The girl insisted, "That's what they told me in court. I deserted him. And I'm the one who has the job. Twenty-five bucks I gave the bastard last month."

The boy advised, "Take the court to court. What's your job?"

She picked her pimples. "I baby-sit."

He said, "Sweet."

She kissed him at the front of his neck. "Will you ball me? I ain't no virgin."

Too sad to intervene, Doktor Tschisch headed for the kiosk at the corner. Perhaps he'd purchase some candies for his lovers. A small customer no more than twelve was chafing with the cooped-up vendor, an old hand at newspapers and chewing gum.

"You got it all wrong," said the vendor. "It's not whores give you V.D. It's girls. Whores care for themselves. On the average."

The boy wouldn't nibble. "I'm still for my girl. I could have a thousand whores. But I can wait. She'll get out of prison soon."

The vendor's palm flickered, demanding its fee. "Don't be an ass," whispered the man. "Honest. No clap!" Just as Tschisch turned away, the boy handed over five dollar bills.

Tschisch saw that there was a lot of work for him yet. In fact, at the entrance to his building a bum asked him for spare change. But Tschisch was broke, his pockets stuffed with sweets.

The bum chewed his loose teeth. His tongue projected like a fuse. Then, as if a bomb had exploded in him and he was about to lose consciousness, the bum poured out his life story. "I pushed my sons, kicked their faces in, so they should be Kennedys. That's one of them over there. Hanging across the hydrant."

Doktor Tschisch had the sense of danger afoot but did not want to be impolite. "Two patients are waiting for me," he said at last.

The drunk was impressed. "Is that so? What's violence? Do you know?"

Anxious to confront the altered faces of his lovers Doktor Tschisch extended his hands and said, "Goodbye for now."

"Aren't you going to examine me, skipper? I'm out of shape. How about it? At least throw me a pebble. Before the commies take over. How long? Three days? Nobody dictates me, Jake. Come back here!"

The bum was urinating already.

Tschisch's outskirts animal, more ocelot than cat,

stuck his huge face between Tschisch's legs. That was
worth waiting for. If man remembers only evil and
forgets good, let him learn from Tschisch's animal that
there is an other way. Tschisch stooped to kiss his cat.
Then raced upstairs.

The Doktor tapped his front door with his head,
exhausted from his ascent. As he unlocked the reluctant
door and half fell in, his heart almost gave out. Nothing
seemed his anymore. He felt as though wheeled into an
autopsy room. With all his senses, with whatever bits
were left him, he sought his two lovers. Part smelling
their position, part tasting their whereabouts.

It appeared to him that the girl awoke at his coming
after an endless stupor. After she and her man made
perfect love together. After they had touched bottom
and emerged beaming. It sounded to Tschisch as if,
despite the bounty of her love's weight, she shifted to
one side to face their Maker, Doktor or Viktor Tschisch.

"There was something in this for all of us," he
smelled himself say. "Old gheezer like me included!"

At that, Tschisch felt the boy plunge off the girl like
an anchor. As if the girl were now hanging over the
bed's edge like a drunk, whispering, "Love, what's the
matter? Are you hurt?" As if the boy wouldn't answer.
And Doktor Tschisch himself were now thumping the
boy's chest, petting his dead-pan face, scratching his
toes, trying to elicit reflexes like a piano player. But the
boy was no jazz musician to stand for his solo. He
wasn't sticking up for anybody.

Tschisch imagined himself weeping, imagined himself asking the girl, "Remember *my* Father? If he were here he'd say, 'Endocarditis. Elusive case. Embolism. Cerebral hemorrhage. Death could come any time!' Then my Father would have asked the corpse's forgiveness, wiped away his own tears and commenced cutting."

Tschisch dreamt he saw the stunned girl sail onto her lover in a swoop of fury, beating him, shaking him, lifting him, crying, 'Now? Dead? Now?'

Tschisch saw himself crawl toward the opened window, surveying the street for any sign of his cat. Magically the animal materialized. He and the cat exchanged attentivenesses.

Then Tschisch sensed the girl approach him from behind and slam the window against his skull, cracking both temples instantly. Repetition was unnecessary.

In a panic of fear beyond death Tschisch saw the girl return to her lover, again attempting to raise him to his dead feet. Tschisch's agony was more than the Doktor dreamt possible. He understood that the boy would lunge now against the window where he himself lay pinned. And he imagined exactly her instincts too, that she would reopen the window and shove her Doktor eastward like a wheelbarrow until he sank to the absolute south. From his present position Tschisch noticed the puzzled glare of his cat who couldn't follow the rules of his master's complicated game.

Tschisch guessed the girl would end the cat's confusion. He smelled the coming disaster. She embraced her lover for the last occasion. And leaned out together with him as though to exercise both their backs. Once across the fulcrum they dropped. Gracefully as sun and chariot.

According to Tschisch's sense of things it was now as if only his cat survived.

Hence for the first time in his life, Doktor Viktor Tschisch was not certain who he was or what he had accomplished.

FICTION COLLECTIVE

Books in Print